EMMA'S SECRET

A. P. JENSEN

COPYRIGHT

This is a work of fiction. Names, characters, places, and incidents are either the product of the author's imagination or are used fictitiously, and any resemblance to actual persons, living or dead, business establishments, or locales is purely coincidental.

CHAPTER 1

"*W*hat?"

Peter Logan stopped dead in front of a wall of floor to ceiling glass in his office in Seattle. His hand tightened on the phone. He couldn't believe what he was hearing. There was a short pause on the other end.

"Shit. I guess Emma didn't call you while she was there?" Tommy asked.

"She was here for a *week*?"

"I assumed that she would. Are you guys fighting?" Tommy floundered.

Peter went rigid with anger. "We are now. Why the hell would she come to Seattle and not call?"

"How the hell should I know?"

"I gotta go," Peter said and hung up.

He began to dial Emma's cell then decided he wanted to see her expression when he asked her why the hell she didn't call him when she was in Seattle for a week on business. The second bakery she opened with her best friend was a ten-minute walk from his office building. He wasn't taking this well, not when he'd been sitting in his office, thinking of her instead of working. He yearned for her and all the while, she was only a few minutes away. He'd never felt so dismissed in his life. They'd been together almost a year and he hadn't seen her in two months. Did Emma invite him to dinner, ask to see his place or ask to spend the night? No. She reserved a hotel room, spent a week in *his* city and drove back to Bellingham without once dialing his number.

Peter called his driver. "Have my car at the curb in five minutes."

"Yes, sir."

His office door opened and he glared at his business partner, Derek, who took one look at him and held his hands up like a fugitive faced with a machine gun.

"I didn't do it," Derek said.

"I'm leaving for the day," Peter snarled.

Derek's brows flew up. "What do you mean?"

"I mean," Peter said through clenched teeth, "I'm leaving and won't be back until tomorrow."

"Why?"

"I need to see Emma."

Derek looked bewildered. "Who?"

"Emma," Peter growled. "We've been together almost a year and you can't remember her name?"

Derek shrugged. "I remember names when I see a face to go with it. How can I remember a girl I've never met? She's the baker chick, yeah?"

"I have something to sort out with her. I'll be back tomorrow."

"Why are you so ticked?"

Peter shouldered past his business partner and his ever-efficient secretary, Pat.

"Hold all my messages until tomorrow," Peter said and she nodded.

Peter strode through the hallways and saw people duck

into their offices or avert their eyes. He was used to it and right now, he was grateful. He wasn't in the mood to talk to anyone.

"We have that meeting tomorrow morning," Derek said, keeping pace with him.

"I know." Peter tried to keep his voice controlled with effort.

"Just reminding you. I didn't know you were with the baker chick anymore. You haven't seen her in, what? Two months?"

"Keeping tabs on my sex life?"

"Someone has to. Why are you so mad at her?"

"She was in the city for a week and didn't call me," Peter hissed.

Derek mulled that over for a moment. "Well, you haven't seen her for two months. Maybe she thinks you're not together. Do you call her?"

Peter shot him a frosty glare. "That's not the point."

Derek shrugged. "Oh, well. Get her out of your system and show up with a smile tomorrow for the meeting. It's a huge one."

"I don't smile," Peter reminded him.

Derek flashed his pearly whites. "Guess it's a good thing I'm your partner then, huh? See you tomorrow."

Peter walked out of the building, took the keys from his driver and revved the engine of his BMW. His temper was at a low-level boil as he made his way out of the city and began the almost two-hour drive to Bellingham, the small town where Emma lived. If Tommy hadn't called, he never would have known Emma came to the city at all. What was wrong with her? Yeah, so it had been two months since he went to see her, but he was busy, damn it. He raked his mind, trying to remember the last time he spoke to her, but his days passed in a jumble of phone calls, emails and paperwork. He couldn't remember the last time he talked to Emma, but that didn't mean he forgot about her. The truth was, he thought about her *too* much, which was the real reason he didn't carve out time in his schedule for her. He'd never felt this attached to a woman and he didn't like it. Instead of feeding his obsession with Emma, he tried to starve it and now... Emma came to Seattle and never once dialed his number.

His anger didn't abate as he entered Bellingham and navigated his way to her neighborhood. He pulled into her driveway as the sun began to set. Her house had a walk around porch, fenced in lawn and lived in feel. He started for the front door, but on a hunch rounded the house. Her house was built into a hill that overlooked a large lake and sure enough, there she sat on her back porch, watching the activity below. She had her feet braced against the railing, but when she caught sight of him, she let out a startled yelp. Deep blue eyes flared wide and her rosebud mouth dropped open in surprise.

"Peter?"

The smile that spread across her face made the angry words he rehearsed disappear. He walked up the back-porch steps and when she got to her feet, he hauled her against him. He tilted her chin up and kissed her. She didn't resist. She let out a sound of pleasure and clasped her hands behind his neck.

Simmering anger morphed into hot desire. He grasped her around the waist and let out a groan when she wrapped her legs around his waist. He shouldered through the back door into the house and moved through the kitchen to the living room. He wasn't going to make it upstairs to the bedroom. His hands shook as they moved over her. He had to have her here, now. He set her on the couch and she didn't resist when he tugged off her shirt and unbuttoned her jeans. When he pulled away to shuck out of his suit, sapphire eyes gleamed with need and he couldn't get rid of their clothes fast enough. They slid from the couch to the floor. When he thrust into her, she arched her back. He brushed kissed over her pale throat and twisted dark strands of her hair around his fist. They burned each other up. When she climaxed, she bit the base of his neck and that sent him over the edge.

~

*W*hile Peter took a shower, Emma called for a pizza delivery and pulled out beers. She sat at the table and jiggled her foot while she waited for him. Her body tingled and she couldn't stop the excitement and anticipation she felt. She hadn't seen Peter in two months and now he showed up out of the blue.

She got back from Seattle only a couple of hours ago. It was a long week in the city while she tended to their second bakery, which was only a couple of months old. All week Emma fiddled with her phone, debating whether to call Peter. The last time she heard from him, he told her he wouldn't be able to make it out to Bellingham because of business. He never rescheduled and she didn't know how to take that.

When they first began to date, Peter visited every other week. Now, she was lucky to see him once every other month. She wondered if this was how he would end their relationship—by not coming back. She knew he wasn't the committed type, so when Peter stopped calling, she came to terms with the fact that he was distancing himself from her and now here he was.

Emma answered the door and carried the steaming pizza to the table as Peter came downstairs. Sex oozed from his pores and even after being with him for almost a year, her mouth watered at the sight of him. There was something about his broody, piercing eyes that made her want to jump him. His eyes moved over her before he grabbed a beer and sat across from her. They ate in companionable silence for a while. They were both ravenous and although she was dying to ask what he was doing here, she didn't want to pressure him. She enjoyed his company and… loved him. He was a friend of her business partner's husband, Tommy. When they were introduced, Emma tried to ignore the chemistry between them, but Peter refused to be dismissed. He wooed her outrageously. Peter arrived in her life at a time when she was going into a downward spiral. He had no idea how badly she needed touch or how he got her through September without falling into depression. She and Peter would make a year next month and his presence gave her hope that she wouldn't be alone again this September. His presence pushed away the nightmares waiting for her in sleep.

"Tommy called me," Peter said.

"Oh, that's nice," Emma said, taken aback by the sharp look he settled on her. "Did he have something bad to tell you?"

Peter took a slow pull from his beer. "Are we fighting?"

Emma blinked. "How can we be fighting? I haven't seen you in months."

Peter's eyes narrowed. "I've been busy."

"You're always busy."

He set his beer bottle down very deliberately. "You were in Seattle and didn't contact me."

Emma sensed the anger in him. Peter was an imposing figure, even when he was dressed only in sweat pants. Strength and determination were imbedded into the lines of his face. It was an aspect of his personality that drew her to him. Right now, his dark eyes were moody and focused on her, but she wasn't intimidated.

She shrugged. "You're always busy. I didn't want to bother you."

A muscle twitched in his jaw. "I'm not too busy for you."

"Then why haven't I seen you for two months?" she asked sweetly.

He took another pull on his beer and her mouth tightened. She didn't want to fight with him, but she wouldn't let him make her feel guilty. How was she supposed to read a man who didn't show his emotions?

"I didn't even know if we were together," she said honestly.

He stared at her. "I never said we were over."

"You never told me we were together either," she tossed back. "What else am I supposed to think? I thought that's how you do this sort of thing—"

She stopped when he held up a hand.

"I don't end things by not coming back," he informed her.

"Well, how am I supposed to know?" she said defensively. "I've never been with a guy like you before."

He frowned. "Like me?"

"I went to the grocery store and saw your face on a magazine."

He shrugged. "That's business."

She tapped her hands on the table. "Is that why you're here? Because Tommy told you I was in the city?"

"You should have called."

She had her pride. She didn't want to leave voicemails that wouldn't be returned. She knew she was out of her league where Peter was concerned. He never asked her to come to Seattle. He always came to Bellingham and she harbored the secret fear that he was embarrassed to introduce her to anyone in that part of his life. She and her best friend and business partner, Anna, were doing well, but she couldn't compare to the business arena Peter played in. She stuffed her insecurities deep down and told herself to enjoy Peter for the time being.

"Things have been crazy at the office, but I'll find time to visit," he said.

She heard it before. She didn't want to hear promises he couldn't keep. She got up from her chair and sat on his lap. He wrapped his arms around her and she tilted her head up for a kiss. Peter didn't disappoint. She soaked in his presence and lost herself in him.

"How long are you here?" she mumbled into her bed sheets several hours later.

"Just tonight. I have a meeting in the morning," Peter said in a rumbly voice.

Her heart gave a painful throb, but when he turned her to face him, she didn't resist.

~

*S*treet lamps lit the bedroom in a dim orange glow. Peter didn't have to look at the clock to know dawn was an hour away. Irritation pushed away his satisfaction. He was still angry. Derek was right. Emma believed that they weren't even together. She lay beside him now with a small, pale hand splayed over his heart. She woke a hunger in him he couldn't sate. He scowled as he examined her peaceful expression, grateful she wasn't awake. Her eyes pierced him to the core and left him feeling stripped and vulnerable.

Peter was torn between having her again or getting away as quick as possible. He and Emma had the kind of relationship he always wanted—mutual companionship, no strings. It was understood that they were exclusive. Even though he didn't like clingy women, he expected Emma to call. It was what he came to expect from past relationships but Emma, as usual, wasn't acting like the others. Was he a hypocrite for wanting her to act like a *normal* woman in a relationship? He never wanted a woman to demand things from him, so why was he agitated that Emma didn't try to put strings on him? Emma never asked for anything.

He glanced around the room filled with old wooden chests, hand painted drawers and fresh flowers on the nightstand. He wasn't sure when his mind decided this was home rather than the high rise he bought for an outrageous amount in Seattle. As far as he could tell, Emma wasn't trying to keep or lose him. She enjoyed his company and never pushed for more. Being around Emma brought to life a part of him he didn't know existed—a basic yearning to be needed, to belong to someone. He hated it. Emma accomplished what other women failed to do. She distracted him from business and had more power over him than he would admit.

She arched against him and he grit his teeth. He pushed down the need that arose and pulled away. It was probably best he was going back to the city. He needed to clear his head. He was fine before Emma came into his life. He couldn't figure out why a small-town business owner with blue eyes turned him into a man filled with unrelenting need.

≈

*E*mma woke when Peter rose from the bed. She opened one eye to watch his well-defined body walk into the bathroom. A moment later, the shower came on. She sighed and rolled onto her back. Damn Peter's internal clock. She'd been hoping he would postpone his trip back to the city for at least three more hours, but business always came first.

Peter loved her through the night as if he couldn't get

enough of her and now he would go and act as if nothing happened. Again. She tried not to be irritated by his eagerness to leave, but what was she supposed to think? Was he trying to keep things casual between them or was he such a workaholic that he couldn't bear to be away from his business? Either way she looked at it, Peter made sure she didn't depend on him. Peter hadn't given her false promises and she respected that. She didn't need a man who said all the right things, but when hard times came, was nowhere to be found. She already learned that lesson the hard way. Two years ago, she vowed she would never beg anyone to stay.

She reached for a robe and headed into the kitchen. She started the preparations for an omelet. Her mind drifted to their fast approaching one-year anniversary… and the other anniversary that haunted her. Did Peter know they were coming up on a year? She let out a snort. Probably not. What she had with him wasn't technically a relationship, but she didn't focus on that. In some ways, they were alike—guarded workaholics that stayed away from the emotional stuff. She couldn't point the finger at Peter because her life was dominated by work as well, which is why their relationship worked. Work had become her coping mechanism and it paid off when she and Anna opened a second bakery in the city.

Her landline phone rang as she beats the eggs. She glanced at the clock, 5:15am. Emma squinted at the unfamiliar number on the screen. She let the phone ring and continued to whip eggs as the answering machine clicked and a voice she hadn't heard in almost two years filled the kitchen. Her body turned to ice and the bowl of eggs splattered over the tile when her fingers contracted.

"Emma, it's me, Ben. I know it's been a long time, but I need to talk to you. You haven't answered any of my letters or calls. I know what I did was unforgivable. I know that, but… I still love you. I can't help it. I'm sorry, Em. You have my number. Please, call me. Bye."

The only sound in the kitchen was Emma's rapid breathing. She wasn't aware of Peter calling her name until he swung her around. She stared at him blankly for several moments.

"You look like you're gonna pass out." Peter pushed her into a chair and crouched in front of her. "Who the hell is Ben?"

She shook her head, unable to speak. How *dare* Ben call after all this time? Tears pricked her eyes. She was pissed that Ben had the power to make her feel this way after all this time. She screwed her eyes shut and fought for control.

"You need to talk, baby. Who is he?" Peter couldn't keep the anger out of his voice.

"He's not important," she said through stiff lips.

"You're white as a sheet. Try again. He's your ex?"

She nodded. When she opened her eyes, she saw that Peter's face was stiff with tension. He placed big hands on her thighs and rubbed up and down.

"How long has it been since you've seen him?"

"Years," she whispered.

She knew why he was calling. The anniversary of the worst night of her life was coming up and Ben was a part of it.

"Do you want me to call the cops?" Peter pushed.

She shook her head.

"What did he do to you?"

She closed her eyes. She and Peter never brought up their pasts and she hated that Ben caused this. She couldn't talk to anyone about it, not even her best friend, Anna.

Peter's cell rang. He let out a low growl and snatched it from the suit jacket draped over the chair. She was grateful for the interruption. She finally noticed the eggs oozing over the floor and began to wipe it up with a dishcloth.

"Damn it, Derek, I know what time it is. I'm on my way," Peter snapped.

Emma wrung the dishcloth under hot water and grabbed a cleaner and sprayed the spot on the floor as Peter finished his angry conversation with Derek. She kept her head down as she wiped in circles, still rattled by Ben's call.

"Emma?"

She grunted and continued to clean. She let out a startled yelp when he hauled her up and pushed her into the chair again. He tossed the soaked dishrag in the sink and crouched in front of her again.

"Is there something I should know about Ben?" he asked.

"No."

"Are you afraid of him?"

Emma shook her head. "No. It just… didn't end well."

His eyes moved over her face. She looked away because she didn't want him to see how shaken she really was. She didn't want to talk about Ben.

"I have to go."

"I know." *Just leave*, she thought. *Just leave me alone so I can put myself back together again.*

"If he bothers you, let me know, okay?"

She nodded, though she'd never do such a thing. This was between her and Ben. She wouldn't bring Peter into it. As if he could hear her thoughts, he frowned.

"I don't want to leave you like this. You look…" he trailed off and closed a hand over hers. "You're cold."

"It's a shock hearing from him after all this time."

Peter rubbed her hands between his. "He said he loves you."

"We've known each other since we were kids."

There was so much history between her and Ben. She

loved him once upon a time, but now the sound of his voice made her throat tighten with the need to scream. She felt ill. The nasty taste of betrayal permeated her mouth.

Peter's hands tightened on her. "Do you want to see him?"

"No."

There was no hesitation in her voice and he relaxed.

"You broke it off with him?"

"Yes."

"Are you gonna be okay?"

"Yes."

He leaned forward and kissed her. The heat of him chased away the chill for the moment and brought back memories of their night together. He brushed her hair back from her face and her hands fisted in his shirt before she realized what she was doing.

"Tell Ben you're with me," Peter growled. "I'll see you soon."

He shrugged into his suit jacket, kissed her once more and walked out the front door. She watched him from the doorway as he unlocked his BMW.

"When will you be back?"

The words flew out of her mouth before she could stop herself. She wanted to be alone, but she wanted—*needed* to know he would be back. He paused and looked every inch the tycoon he was. His fancy suit didn't fit in well with her fence that needed to be painted and the modest homes around him.

"When do you want me?"

"September fourteenth."

She waited for him to recognize the date, but there was no comprehension on his face. He gave her an unreadable look before he nodded and ducked into the car. She waved as he drove away before she locked the front door and slid to the floor. She covered her face with shaking hands and wept.

CHAPTER 2

*P*eter moved through the crowd of men in tuxedos and women in daring dresses. The people that once laughed in his face wouldn't meet his eyes. Every goal he strived for, he surpassed. He sacrificed everything and came out on top in the business world. Men scrambled to shake Peter's hand and women gave him suggestive glances, but all he felt was a gnawing restlessness. He didn't want to be here. The world he once desperately wanted to be a part of was overrated. He made his way across the room and accepted the flute of champagne thrust into his hand. *All for show*, he thought cynically. He found himself wondering what Emma would think of this crowd and his mouth quirked. She would be disgusted. On the surface, Emma fit into this crowd. She was beautiful, successful and poised but she wasn't a socialite. Emma enjoyed life in her small town.

He walked onto the balcony and took a deep breath. Damp cold settled over him. He glanced up at the sky, but it was too cloudy to see anything. His cell phone seemed unnaturally heavy in his pocket. He called Emma twice since he left a month ago. She sounded like her normal self, but he knew something was wrong. When he asked if she had any more calls from Ben, she said no and changed the subject. He wanted to push, but she never asked about his past, so what right did he have to pry? He tried to clear his schedule to see her, to pin down *exactly* what her relationship with Ben had been, but a lucrative client came knocking on his door. Since then he practically lived in his office, working day and night to ensure everything was perfect.

"My father is very impressed with you."

Peter didn't have to turn to know that Leslie, the daughter of his new client, joined him on the balcony. He'd seen her maybe twice in the past month and she made no secret of her willingness to take their acquaintance to the next level.

"He wouldn't have hired me otherwise," Peter replied.

"Your story is legendary. I think a big reason he hired you is because he knows you don't give up. You're too stubborn. You wouldn't be here otherwise."

His rags to riches story had been publicized when he got his first big break in the business world. Coming from nothing made him ruthless. He had nothing to lose. Sheer iron will made him rise to the top.

"Do you know how sexy you look in that suit?" Leslie asked in a husky voice that made her sound like she had a cold.

He was cynical enough to know making millions made him more attractive than he used to be when he made minimum wage.

"My girlfriend tells me all the time," Peter said blandly.

That was a flat out lie. Emma stared at him like he was from another planet when he arrived on her doorstep in a suit. She didn't ask about his life in the city and never once asked how much he was worth. Emma was a savvy business-woman that enjoyed her simple life. He appreciated that about her. Maybe it was part of the reason he'd been attracted to her in the first place. She was confident, passionate, easygoing, smart and didn't play games.

"Why isn't she here guarding you?"

Leslie fluttered fake lashes and eased closer as if the proximity would influence him to change his mind. In the past, it probably would have. Leslie was beautiful, but she was also calculating and cold.

"I can take care of myself," Peter said.

She looked him up and down with admiring eyes. "Yes, you can. You're one of the most eligible bachelors in the city. Don't you want to experience *all* the city has to offer?"

Leslie sidled closer. Her perfume was light and delicate. He barely suppressed an irritated growl. Didn't she know he could see through her guise? If he was smart enough to make it this far, he was intelligent enough to see a gold digger when he saw one.

"I've sampled my fair share. I'm content," he said.

Leslie looked horrified. "You're not going to marry her, are you?"

The question threw him for a moment. He couldn't imagine being married. "No."

Leslie relaxed and her coy smile returned. "I thought not. You can't marry a nobody. Who is she? I've never seen her in any pictures with you."

"She doesn't like the spotlight," he said with a shrug.

"What kind of woman lets you go solo in the city?" Leslie asked, bewildered. If she had Peter Logan, she wouldn't let him out of her sight. "You need a wife that can host parties for you, someone who can handle your clients."

"And you think you're qualified?" Peter asked with grim humor.

"I'm perfect," she breathed.

Before Peter could reply, Derek appeared and Leslie

turned her high wattage smile on him. After all, he was just as wealthy as Peter, but Leslie preferred Peter's broodiness. Derek was known for his one-night conquests and would never marry. Peter, on the other hand, might take the plunge one day. Why shouldn't it be with her?

"Your father's looking for you, Leslie," Derek said.

"Is he? I'd better go. Peter, call me," Leslie said and blew him a kiss before she sashayed away.

Derek waited until Leslie was out of sight before he asked, "Why'd she corner you and not me?"

"She thinks I'm in the market for a wife," Peter said.

Derek flinched. "She doesn't look mad, whatever you told her."

"I used Emma as a defense."

"Well, you shackled yourself to her, figuratively. Want to go out to a club to celebrate?"

Peter glanced at his watch. "No. I have work to do."

"Work?" Derek threw his hands up in the air. "We finalized the deal yesterday and you want to leave the party to work? You're starting to worry me."

"Don't. I'm fine."

Peter couldn't even begin to tell his friend what was going on with him because he didn't understand it himself. The suit he wore, although perfectly tailored, seemed too stiff and confining. Every day, he poured over his computer, reassured clients and spent half the day talking on the phone. There were always emails and responsibilities and they distracted him from Emma.

Ever since he came back from his impromptu trip, he couldn't stop thinking about her. He wanted to know why she looked gutted when she heard Ben's voice. She was always so cheerful when he was around that it rocked him to see her pale, shaking and tearful. He really didn't know anything about her past and she damn well never mentioned

17

a guy named Ben. Were there more "Ben's" that he didn't know about?

The urge he felt to stay and comfort her that day surprised him. He wasn't the type to save damsels in distress and the urge to offer emotional support was alien to him. He never met his father and his mom was a drunk that handed him off to an aunt who could care less about his existence. He was a hard man because he had to be and no woman had ever crept past his guards except Emma. She tried to hide how shaken she was by the phone call, but she hadn't asked him to stay. He wanted Emma with a force that shouldn't surprise him, but still did. The strength of his desire was beginning to worry him. It didn't abate since the last time he saw her, it had grown. She called him a week ago and... Something niggled at the back of his memory, but Derek interrupted his line of thought.

"The doctor said you should take it easy," Derek said, watching him closely.

"I am," Peter said with a shrug.

"Whatever. Just don't overdo it," Derek groused.

Four hours later, Peter settled in his desk chair. The empty office building allowed him to focus easily. There were no ringing phones or chattering voices to block out. It was just him and the work.

He glanced out of the floor to ceiling window behind his desk. Seattle was beautiful at night. He eyed the building across the street and knew he should go to his penthouse. It was a five-minute walk, but... why should he go home? A picture of Emma's face appeared in his mind and he tensed. He pushed her out of his mind and tried to convince himself that the reason he didn't want to go to the penthouse was because he had work to do, but he knew the real reason—he wasn't getting much sleep without her.

≈

*H*e wasn't coming. Emma sat on the couch in her living room, legs tucked under her. A perfect white slice of cheesecake, Peter's favorite, sat sullenly on the coffee table before her. For the third time, she rang his cell but the call went straight to voicemail. The low level hurt that hummed through her all day turned sharp and dug deeper. She set the phone down very carefully and examined the dessert for any imperfections, but there were none.

She called Peter a week ago to remind him to come back to Bellingham on the fourteenth. He said he would be at her house by seven. She deliberately hadn't mentioned their one-year anniversary, waiting to see if he would remember, but he forgot about her completely. Emma glanced at the clock, now on its way to eleven. She looked down at the lingerie she and Anna picked out and swallowed back the tears.

The silence of the house pressed in on her. On nights when loneliness crept into her heart, she imagined she could hear the echo of her parents talking and laughing in the kitchen. The fantasy lulled her into a false sense of peace, but tonight pain ruled out all else. She pushed away the melancholy and guilt by focusing her attention on her anniversary with Peter, all to no avail.

This showed in no uncertain terms what position she held in Peter's life. He promised he would come back and here she was, waiting for him on their anniversary. Emma couldn't understand how Peter remembered every business contact, but he couldn't remember a simple dinner request from her. Each time he pushed something back for business, Emma shrugged off the hurt, but tonight was different. Tonight, it mattered. Emma couldn't stop the tears. From the beginning, she knew not to rely on him too much, that letting herself fall for him would be monumentally stupid, but she didn't listen. It wasn't just that he forgot their anniversary, it was… everything.

Her business partner Anna and her husband Tommy loved each other. It was the way her father looked at her mother. She was sure it wasn't how Peter looked at her. He probably viewed their relationship as a convenient one. She had too, at first. But she cared about him and missed him. She worked more and more to distract herself from their mockery of a relationship—arriving at the bakery at three in the morning to help Anna bake and staying until six at night or until Anna kicked her out. When she dragged herself to this quiet house, she found herself wishing for a normal relationship with someone who demanded she get her ass home. Her relationship with Peter was bound to end sometime. She hadn't pressured him for fear of scaring him off, yet it seemed their affair had run its course. She knew he wouldn't offer more. Was his absence deliberate or had he genuinely forgotten their date?

The cursive on the rim of the plate, which spelled *Happy Anniversary* drooped as the chocolate syrup melted. *Just as well*, Emma thought. She put the dessert in the fridge and paused to blow out the candles around the room before she walked upstairs. She shucked the expensive lingerie and pulled on a tank top and sweats. She turned away from his empty side of the bed and cried herself to sleep.

CHAPTER 3

*A*nna leaned against the doorjamb to Emma's office, yawning and drinking out of a mug that said, *I'm the boss.*

"You're supposed to be at home recovering from having wild sex all night."

Anna narrowed her eyes as Emma rubbed a hand over bloodshot eyes and pushed away from the computer. Anna, a petite red head with a lot of spunk had a sixth sense where Emma was concerned. Emma kept so much hidden that Anna had to use every ounce of intuition she possessed to figure out when something was wrong. Right now, her senses were screaming that all wasn't well with her best friend and business partner.

"I thought I'd come in early and finish some paperwork," Emma said, avoiding eye contact.

Anna raised her brows and glanced at her bare wrist. "Honey, the sun isn't even up. How long have you been here?"

Emma didn't answer. Anna moved around the desk and put her arms around her friend. Emma's eyes stung with tears. Anna and Emma attended culinary school for two years before Emma decided she was more interested in business. They came together to open a bakery. Emma did the finances while Anna took care of the kitchen. They were closer than sisters and Anna was all she had left.

"It's that time of year again, isn't it?" Anna murmured. "Are you having a hard time because of the date or did Peter do something to ruin the perfect night we planned?"

Emma let out a shaky breath. "Both, I guess. He didn't show. I think he forgot."

Anna jerked up so fast, she nearly strangled Emma.

"He *what*?" Anna asked in a low voice of doom.

Emma sighed. "It's okay, Anna."

Anna stared at her incredulously. "It's not okay. I'm going to kick his sorry ass!"

"I'm going to end it, so there's no need to get upset."

Emma turned away from her friend. She didn't see the shocked, alarmed expression that crossed Anna's face.

"End it? As in, break up with him?" Anna stammered.

"It's time."

Anna held up her hand. "Time out."

Anna rushed out of the room and returned a minute later with a caramel mocha for Emma and her favorite scone. She set it in front of her friend.

"Eat. Drink," Anna ordered.

Obediently, Emma drank and felt warmth spread through her cold hands. She took a bite of the scone and sipped more coffee. The headache she'd been ignoring for an hour began to ease. Anna sat in a chair across from Emma, watching her like a hawk.

"Okay, spill," Anna ordered.

"There's nothing to say."

"Let me get this straight. He didn't show up for your one-year anniversary so you're going to break up with him?"

Emma frowned. "You make it sound stupid."

"It's not stupid, but you're emotional. Peter's an asshole, but don't you think breaking up with him is going a little overboard?"

"No, I don't. It's more than that."

Anna tilted her head to the side expectantly.

"You're not going to leave me alone, are you?" Emma asked, exasperated

"Nope. So, why are you breaking up with him? Is there more going on that you're not telling me?"

Emma's rosebud mouth tightened. "I want more and Peter can't offer that. We've been together a year and not once has either of us tried to push for more. He's in the city most of the time and when he remembers me," she said with a bitter smile, "he stays for the weekend and it's great, but…" Emma shook her head. "I want a guy like Tommy that adores me."

"Peter cares for you, Emma."

Anna felt compelled to defend Peter because she'd seen the way he watched Emma. Even Tommy, who tried to dissuade Peter at Anna's behest, admitted he'd never seen Peter focus on any woman the way he had with Emma. The few times Peter and Emma attended a party, the chemistry between them was undeniable. Unlike her and Tommy who were opposites, Emma and Peter were so alike, they melded together. The only thing they truly differed in was style. Peter was modern and high end while Emma preferred homemade simplicity. Anna didn't understand their relationship, but hadn't pushed since Emma hadn't made a single complaint… until now.

"Peter cares, but I need more than that. I love him." Emma's eyes were so sad that Anna looked away. "But, that isn't enough, is it?"

Anna winced. "You love him?"

Emma smiled wanly. "I'm an idiot. He has heartbreaker written all over him."

"You're not an idiot. He is. Are you sure you want to end it? This is a hard time of year for you."

Emma ignored Anna's reference to the other anniversary she was desperately trying not to remember. "Anna, I felt like a fool. I dressed up in sexy lingerie for a man who never showed. How pathetic is that? I'm an afterthought to him. I know he's busy, but I can't keep doing this. I want someone who has me somewhere in the top three of their priority list. I don't think I'm even in his top ten."

Anna nodded thoughtfully and didn't comment.

Emma ran her hands through her hair. "Sometimes I think he loves me and sometimes I think he's on the brink of asking for more, but then he shuts down and goes back to the city and shows up again weeks later. What am I supposed to think?"

"Wait until I talk to Tommy," Anna muttered.

"This has nothing to do with Tommy," Emma argued. "This is between Peter and I. I have emotions, needs…" Her voice wavered and she had to stop to compose herself. "I'm human and I want a man who will hold me even when I don't ask. I need a man who will stand by me. Ben walked away when I needed him most. It gutted me." Emma tilted her chin up. "I can't stay with a guy who doesn't need anyone. I want a *real* relationship."

"I hear you, sister," Anna said, shaking her head.

"I called Peter several times and it went straight to voice-mail. I doubt if he has any inkling about our anniversary. I want someone that cares about that, you know?"

"What was his excuse?" Anna demanded angrily.

"I didn't leave a message. I doubt he even remembers we had a date last night." Emma waved a shaking hand. "It doesn't matter. I want space right now anyway."

"You deserve a great guy," Anna said. "But I don't think Peter's going to take this as easy as you think."

"He only remembers me when he wants sex. He'll move onto someone else, if he hasn't already."

Anna watched Emma shut down emotionally as she turned back to her computer. Emma's long black hair was mussed and her normally sparkling blue eyes were dull. Anna had been counting on Peter to pull Emma through this time of year, the bastard. Anna considered her friend. Emma was a private person and Peter probably had no idea about the details of Emma's parent's death, but that didn't excuse him for breaking his promise. Anna didn't know what to say to comfort her friend and silently damned Peter Logan for hurting her.

~

The office building was filled to capacity with chattering employees and the smell of strong coffee. Peter still wore the same suit from the party the night before. He was exhausted, but grimly satisfied with the progress he made on the portfolio he was building for the new client.

"There's a man named Tommy on the phone for you, sir," Pat said over the intercom.

Peter frowned. "Put it through." When he heard his friend on the phone he said, "Why aren't you calling me on my cell?"

"Your cell is off, jackass," Tommy replied.

Peter looked around the office, wondering where he left it. "I must have put it down somewhere and the battery died."

"The only reason I'm calling is because you're in trouble," Tommy continued.

Peter stopped rummaging through the papers on his desk. "What?"

"Anna yelled at me for introducing you to Emma."

Peter tensed. He knew Anna was overprotective of Emma. Anna filled the role usually reserved for a mother and pulled Peter aside to have a talk with him when he started dating her best friend. He couldn't stop the chill of alarm ripple down his spine. Anna wasn't to be trifled with.

"What happened? What did I do?" he asked

"Apparently, it's what didn't happen. What I deduced from Anna is you missed something huge."

The feeling that he'd forgotten something returned full blast. He leaned against the window and looked down at the busy street below. "Damn, I was supposed to meet Emma at her house last night."

"I'd give her a few days," Tommy advised. "How many times have you done this?" When Peter didn't answer, Tommy clucked his tongue. "I don't know why Emma stayed with you this long. Anna would have divorced me."

"Emma understands how busy I am," Peter said and ignored the way his gut clenched.

On a night when he could have been with Emma, he drank champagne with faceless people and spent all night staring at a computer instead. Missing their date was bad, but not horrible. He would make it up to her.

"Women only understand up to a certain point. From what Anna says, you're close to your quota with Emma," Tommy said.

Peter rubbed his eyes. "Emma isn't Anna, thank God."

"They're best friends. They have more in common than you think."

"Thanks for the head's up. I'll call her."

Peter hung up with Tommy and finally spotted his cell on the floor. It was off. He picked it up and hit Emma's number on speed dial. Her phone went straight to voicemail.

"Hey Emma, I'm sorry about last night. I'll make it up to you. Call me back," he said and hung up.

He tried to get back to work, but he couldn't concentrate. Emma's cell was always on and she usually called him back within the hour. He couldn't shake the feeling that he was missing something. Three hours went by. After five more calls, he rang the bakery and was told by a giggly clerk that Emma wasn't there. He crammed a briefcase with papers, transferred files to his laptop and headed out of the office. He jumped into his BMW and gunned the engine as he headed out of Seattle. Emma was obviously angry. He hadn't seen her in over a month and despite the fact that she was ignoring him, he felt his heart lift at the thought of seeing her. His phone rang twenty minutes into the drive and he glanced at it, hoping it was Emma. It wasn't.

"Where the hell are you?" Derek shouted.

"I'm going to Bellingham. I need to sort out something with Emma."

"I need you here! We have work to do!" Derek snapped.

Peter kept a hold on his temper. "I sorted out the biggest details. I have my laptop and I'll be working while I'm there."

"What's wrong with you? You belong here in the city with me, our business and all these fine women," Derek ranted.

"I need to see Emma."

"Baker chick is messing up your game."

"She's not messing up anything. You're lucky I have her or we'd be in a boxing ring right now."

Derek snorted. "Fine. You like her or whatever. I have a great idea. Why don't you bring her to the city so you don't have to leave?"

"If you have to reach me, email me."

"I don't know what's with you. First Tommy gets married

and moves to Bellingham and now you're visiting once a month for the baker chick. What's the world coming to?"

Peter hung up and relaxed into the luxurious leather. He was exhausted. All he wanted to do was crawl into bed beside Emma and sleep for a week. He didn't want to think anymore. He wanted rest and Emma. He parked in her driveway and grabbed the spare key beneath a ceramic frog in a flowerpot. He unlocked the door and called her name. He glanced at his watch. Two thirty. He would wait for her. He glanced into the living room and frowned. Something looked different, but damned if he could put his finger on it. He walked into the kitchen to see if Emma had beer. He opened the fridge and froze with his hand outstretched when he saw the plate of cheesecake. The chocolate writing on the edge of the plate was smeared, but still legible.

"Shit," he said and thumped his head on the fridge.

CHAPTER 4

*E*mma blinked at the computer screen, stretched and left the office. She walked to the front of the bakery where bursts of laughter distracted her from dark thoughts. She pushed through the double doors and came out behind the counter where several employees chatted with regulars while boxing up pastries and cakes. She smiled when several locals called out to her, but her eyes rounded with joy when she saw a familiar face enter the bakery.

"Georgina!"

Emma embraced Georgina who was dressed in a stylish white pantsuit. Georgina hugged her fiercely and reached out with a blind hand for the man standing off to the side.

"Emma, this is my fiancé, Leo. Leo, this is one of my bridesmaids and best friends from high school, Emma."

Emma beamed at him. "Nice to meet you."

"I warned you about Emma," Georgina said to her fiancé who nodded.

"Warned him?" Emma repeated, confused.

"I told him you used to steal all the attention from Anna

and me in high school. It was bad for our self-esteem," Georgina laughed.

"If that's so, explain why Anna's married and you're soon to be and I'm not?"

Georgina shrugged. "You're picky."

When Emma's mouth opened and closed soundlessly, Georgina took the opportunity to launch into an account of Leo's dramatic proposal. Georgina's dream moment happened in a hot air balloon after three months of dating.

"It's fate." Georgina gushed.

Emma glanced at the so far silent man beside Georgina who didn't take his eyes off his future wife. Leo looked so content listening to Georgina, just being around her. Emma tried to imagine Peter looking at her that way and inwardly snorted. She couldn't imagine Peter proposing publicly, much less so outrageously. Emma felt a pang of envy and instantly shoved it down.

"I remember Anna talking about having a bakery one day and here it is. It's amazing." Georgina said.

Emma smiled. "We took a risk and it paid off. Business is good."

Georgina flapped manicured nails. "That's great. You won't believe whom I ran into! Sam Belissimo! He's a cop now!" She sent Emma a sly look and turned to her fiancé. "Leo, do you mind getting me something to drink?"

He leaned down and gave her a soft kiss before wandering to the counter.

"He didn't ask what you wanted," Emma observed.

Georgina chuckled. "He knows how I like my coffee. Anyway, whatever happened to you and Sam? He's still hot."

Emma laughed. She dated Sam in the seventh grade. "We're just friends, Gina."

Georgina waggled her brows. "What about Travis? I thought I heard a rumor about you and him."

Emma shook her head, amazed. "You left the day we graduated from high school, but you seem caught up on my sex life. How can that be?"

Georgina giggled like a schoolgirl. "My mom keeps tabs on my friends for me. So, who are you with?"

"Who says I'm with someone?"

Emma watched Leo shake out two sugar packets and a careful amount of cream into Georgina's coffee. Did Peter know how she liked her coffee?

"Oh, please, Emma. Guys throw themselves in your path." Georgina accepted the coffee from Leo with a, "Thanks, baby."

Georgina took a sip of her coffee and closed her eyes in bliss before she focused on Emma again. She raised her brows expectantly.

"Well?" A quick search of Emma's face and then a cautious, "Ben?"

Emma's smile disappeared. She swallowed hard as the memories she'd been trying to suppress all day grabbed her by the throat. Georgina realized her blunder and squeezed Emma's hand in apology.

"I'm sorry, Em."

Emma mustered a smile as her stomach pitched. "No. Um, I'm with someone else."

Looking relieved, Georgina beamed and sipped her coffee. "Anyone I know?"

She *really* didn't want to talk about Peter, but she didn't want to talk about Ben so, "No. He lives in the city."

Georgina cocked her head to the side. "What's his name?"

God, why? Emma thought in a silent scream. Here she was talking to her friend about a guy she was about to break up with. "Peter Logan."

Georgina choked on her coffee. Leo patted her on the

back, alarmed. Georgina caught her breath and gaped at Emma.

"Excuse me?"

Emma shifted uncomfortably. "You've heard of him?"

"Uh, yeah! We live in Seattle too! In fact, my Dad does business with him. Everybody's heard of Peter Logan! My God. You've got him."

Emma's heart lurched. "No, not really."

"He was your first adult crush," Leo said.

Emma held up a hand. "Wait. You two have known each other six months and you know how she takes her coffee and who her *adult* crush is?"

"Of course. We talk," Georgina said with a chuckle. "That's what couples do."

"What's her favorite flower?" Emma asked Leo.

"Orchid."

"My God," Emma breathed. "You're perfect!"

Emma embraced Leo, happy that the guy Georgina was set on marrying was thoughtful, caring and authentic. Where did Anna and Georgina find men like this?

"Stop trying to distract me, Emma. Why the hell didn't you tell me you were dating Mr. Dark and Broody?"

Emma shrugged. "It just happened."

"It just happened," Georgina mimicked, eyes sharpening. "And how long have you been dating?"

"We just made a year."

Emma didn't miss Georgina's quick glance down at her ring less finger. Georgina gave her a hopeful expression and Emma felt her heart twist.

"We're taking things slow," Emma said with a forced smile.

Georgina grilled Emma about her longtime obsession with Peter Logan. The more questions Georgina asked, the more puzzled she seemed by Emma's relationship with Peter.

Georgina knew more about Peter from magazine articles than Emma did. Emma's already precarious mood became gloomier by the second. Sensing all was not well, Leo steered the conversation to their upcoming wedding instead. Emma sent him a grateful smile.

"Is Peter your date to my wedding?" Georgina demanded.

A lump formed in Emma's throat. "No, I don't think so."

"Well, he has a little over a month to clear his schedule," Georgina said. "We're here to do some last-minute organizing. We'll probably be driving out on the weekends to finalize wedding details. Is Anna here? She told me she has a sketch of the wedding cake!"

Emma led them into the back room. There was a lot of screeching as Anna and Georgina hugged and gushed over wedding plans. Emma stood off to the side, trying her utmost to appear normal. Anna caught sight of Emma and distracted Georgina by showing her the sketch of the wedding cake before she pushed Emma out the back door.

"Go home. Get some sleep. You look like hell," Anna said before she slammed the door in her face.

Emma heard Georgina rave over the sketch. It should have lifted her mood since she designed it, but her heart wasn't in it. Emma drove to the grocery store and bought two bouquets of the brightest flowers she could find. She parked on the side of the road and tried to get a grip on herself before she carried the bouquets through the graveyard to her parent's tombstones.

The air was chilly and there was no one in sight. It was a cloudy day and the trees rustled as she walked beneath them. She sank to her knees beside the graves of her parents. She lay the flowers over the cold stone with shaking hands. Today made two years since her parent's death. The pain left her breathless. She had no blood relatives and if it hadn't been for Anna, she wasn't sure she would have weathered the storm. Tears streamed down her face. A scream built in her chest, but she refused to let it out. She bent her head, wrapped her arms around herself and rocked.

On the first anniversary of her parent's death she met Peter. She was caught in a haze of depression when he shoved his way into her life. His presence forced her out of grieving and brought her solidly into the present. She loved him even more for that. Peter had been visiting Tommy while he took a break from work. He invaded her life, house and bed and she'd been more than willing. He chased away the dark memories and he got her through September, the worst time of the year for her. She'd been counting on him to be here for *their* anniversary so she didn't have to think about the other one...

Emma lay on the cold, damp grass beside the graves, body curled around them protectively.

"I miss you," she whispered. "Forgive me."

One hand plucked at blades of grass as tears continued to leak from her eyes. She tucked an arm beneath her head and closed her eyes. She listened to the distant sound of the cars passing on the highway and the breeze that swept through the graveyard. When she wasn't at the bakery and couldn't stand being in her empty house, she came here.

Emma wasn't sure how much time passed, but she roused when she heard the sound of running feet. Someone shouted her name and hands pushed her onto her back.

"Emma?" a male voice said in alarm.

Emma opened swollen eyes and stared wearily up at a ruggedly handsome guy with short-cropped blonde hair. He crouched beside her in black jeans and sweater. Muscles rippled beneath his shirt as he took off mirrored sunglasses, revealing worried misty green eyes.

"Ben?"

～

*E*mma drove one handed since Ben cradled her other in his lap. He wrote words on her palm with his finger, a habit he started when they dated in middle school. He spelled "happy" on her palm and she glanced at him, only to find him staring intently out at the moonlit road. He'd done it unconsciously. Ben was her first crush, boyfriend, kiss and more. They dated from intermediate through high school, but went their own way after graduation. Ben stayed in Bellingham while she and Anna headed off to culinary school. When she and Anna returned to open up the bakery, Ben was their first customer.

Emma's parents sang off key with the radio in the back seat. She and Ben chimed in every now and then. Emma grinned like a fool as she navigated the car on the winding road back into town. Headlights from the car behind glinted on the diamond ring on her left finger. She couldn't believe she was engaged. She had it all —family, career and soul mate. What more could she ask for?

"So," Emma's mom said, poking Ben's shoulder. "When are you two going to put us out of our misery and set a date?"

Emma glanced at her mom in the rearview mirror. "Mom, you know I want everything to be perfect!"

Ben rolled his eyes at her parents. "I would marry Emma at the courthouse, but between her and Anna, it's impossible. They have a wedding planner the size of a dictionary."

"Anna would kill me if I get married at a courthouse. Plus, we just acquired the space for the second bakery in the city and—" Emma began.

Emma's mom threw her hands up in the air while her father leaned forward and patted her on the shoulder.

"That's my baby. Always ten steps ahead of everybody else."

"She's gonna work herself into an early grave!" Her mom protested. "Ben, the first things you need to do as Emma's husband is throw away her planner. She has everything so planned out, she'll drive you crazy. I had to train her father to have fun-"

"Hey!" he protested.

"It's true," she continued blithely. "He'd be a workaholic if I let him."

"Better run, Ben," Emma said archly.

Ben raised her hand to his lips and kissed her palm. "Never."

The mood in the car was merry and light. Emma concentrated on the narrow, twisting road. On her right side was a solid wall of rock covered in vines. On the opposite side of the road was a cliff lined with a flimsy fence.

As her parents giggled like lovesick teenagers in the back seat, Ben leaned towards her.

"Em, when are we going to get married?"

"I told you, I'm not sure yet. I still have to reserve a place and business-wise, it's not a good time right now."

"You can't take a week off to get married?"

She shot him an exasperated glance. "Not right now. We need to plan the wedding and I'm in charge of the second bakery and—"

"This isn't how it's always going to be, right?"

She shot him a level glance. "I don't think so, but I care about my company. I'm going to give it all I've got."

"I know," he said. "You haven't changed, have you?"

"No. I like to plan everything. I'm a rigid stick in the mud."

Ben laughed. "I can't wait to get married. I'm going to convince you to sleep in late and—"

Appalled, Emma took her eyes off the road to stare at him.

Her mom shouted from the back seat. "Emma! Watch out!"

Emma jerked her eyes back to the road just in time to see a car stopped in her lane, hazard lights flashing. There was nowhere to pull off. She was going too fast to avoid the car in front of her.

Emma ripped her hand from Ben's grasp and tried to swerve, but headlights showed another car coming in the opposite direction. She slammed on the brakes and an instant later, the car behind *plowed into them. The horrible sound of screeching metal filled the air. The momentum of the crash stole her breath and her face slammed into the steering wheel. She heard screaming and her seatbelt locked to stop her body from flying through the windshield as both cars crashed into the car with its hazard lights flashing. She held onto the wheel, praying they wouldn't all go over the cliff.*

CHAPTER 5

*H*orrible memories battered her senses. She couldn't tear her eyes from Ben. Her heart pounded with a mixture of love, rage and betrayal. He looked exactly the same and it ripped at her insides. So much changed between them in so little time.

"Are you hurt?" Ben demanded, voice panicked.

"What are you doing here?" Emma's voice was husky from crying.

She was in shock. She hadn't seen him since her parent's funeral. Wounds she thought were healed tore open and bled. Her body began to tremble in reaction and the fury that flashed through her banished the cold.

"You're not hurt?" he repeated.

"No. I fell asleep. What are you doing here?"

The worry on his face faded and he looked towards the tombstones. "I wanted to pay my respects." His face closed off and he ran a shaking hand over his face. "Damn it, you scared me."

She wanted to scream at him, to hit him, but she did nothing. She was afraid if she started, she wouldn't stop. She rose from the grass. It was stupid and childish, but she didn't want him anywhere near her parent's tombstones. Things may have worked out differently if he helped—maybe her mother would still be alive. Her hands clenched into fists and she turned away. Seeing Ben after all this time raked her raw.

"Emma."

She didn't stop. She crossed her arms over her chest and started back on the path that led to where her car was parked. She walked briskly and tried to brush off emotions that bubbled and strained to be set free. She sucked in breaths of cold air and let it swirl around in her chest. She knew she would see him eventually and that moment had finally arrived. She faced him and survived.

"Emma."

A hand closed over her arm. Emma jerked away so violently, she nearly toppled onto the grass. She regained her balance and when she met his eyes, her jaw clenched against the need to rage at him.

"*Don't* touch me," she hissed.

If he left her alone, she could stay in control. Seeing Ben brought up the moment of impact, screams and the image of her parents covered in blood.

"I gave you two years," Ben said, voice rough with his own anger.

Emma stalked up to Ben until their faces were less than six inches from each other. He stiffened, but didn't back away.

"There's not a day that passes where I don't think about it. You think two years is enough time for me to get over losing my parents?"

"I was hoping it would be enough time for you to forgive," he said solemnly.

Emma stared at him, speechless. He cleared his throat and ran his hands through his hair.

"What you needed that night, I couldn't—"

"How can you know what I needed that night?" Emma shouted. "You weren't there! You *left* me." She clasped her hands over her heart, which splintered into pieces all over again. Tears filled her eyes, which pissed her off even more.

"You have to listen to me. I won't say sorry anymore because I've said it too many times in the letters and phone calls you don't answer. I wanted to see you, to talk—"

"Talk about what?" She couldn't stop the way her voice rose and cracked. This man she loved, that she would have given her life to deserted her when she needed him most.

Ben refused to back down. "Emma, I love you. We've known each other all our lives. I know how much you loved your parents."

"You *don't* love me!" She shoved against his chest and he took a step back. "And don't you talk about my parents!"

"You think you're the only one who can't sleep at night?" he shouted angrily. "There was nothing either of us could do."

"You mean there's nothing you *would* do. What if that had been me bleeding in the middle of the road? Would you have walked away from me and said there was nothing you could do?"

He swallowed hard and took a step back. Emma went after him and jabbed him in the chest.

"Instead of me on the pavement it was my mother. I needed you to be there for me! I wanted to stop the blood from gushing out of her." Emma felt bile rise in her mouth. She stopped and bent over, trying to catch her breath.

"She was bleeding too much. She didn't have much time —" he began.

"I already knew my father was gone. You think I needed to hear you tell me my mother only had minutes left? I was covered in her blood. I begged you to help me."

Ben was white as a ghost and though she saw the torment and guilt in his eyes, she couldn't find an ounce of sympathy in her heart.

"You should have been right beside me, supporting me as she died in my arms." Emma swallowed hard. "*I* had to call 911, *I* had to tend to the others in the accident that died that night. You were a mile away, just like that driver that saw it all happen and continued on his way. You *don't* love me."

There was a ragged hole in her heart where her parents and Ben had been. She thought her family was complete and in a matter of minutes, all three of them had been irrevocably taken from her. What Ben did that night destroyed her. Over time, she stitched her heart back together, but seeing Ben tore open the stitches and left her wide open.

"I dream about it every night," she whispered. "I couldn't have done anything different. I could've slammed on the brakes two seconds sooner and we'd still get sandwiched between both cars. The impact from behind still would have taken my dad instantly. My mother would still have bits of metal in her." Her voice broke, but she didn't stop. "I never blamed you for the accident, but I can't forgive you for not helping. Even if my mom only had a minute to live, what would it have cost you to help me push down on her wounds? To slow the way blood gushed out of her? Your job was to be there for support and you did the worst thing possible." Tears poured down her cheeks. "I would give anything to talk to them for a few minutes, to hear them talk and laugh."

She was so drained. She needed someone to hold her and tell her that one day the pain wouldn't make her feel as if she were dying.

"Just stay away Ben," she said hoarsely.

This time, he let her go. Emma slammed her car door and rolled down the windows because she felt suffocated. She needed to talk to someone. She started towards the bakery, but didn't want the staff to see her this way. She didn't want their pity. Emma turned towards home, miserable, grief stricken and horribly lonely. Emma's heart skipped a beat when she saw Peter's BMW in the driveway. Regret, love and need balled in her stomach. She was too upset to think about their impending breakup. Right now, she needed him. Nothing else mattered.

Even as she pushed open her car door, Peter came onto the porch. He wore a white dress shirt and slacks. He looked out of place on her well-worn porch, but she didn't care. Emma ran to him. She saw the surprise on his face, but he didn't hesitate when she hurled herself at him. She buried her face against his chest and he held her tight, just the way she needed.

"What's going on?"

She shook her head and he carried her into the house. When he tried to take her into the living room, she spoke up.

"Upstairs."

He hesitated. "Are you sick?"

"Just take me upstairs."

She clutched him because he was the only thing keeping her anchored. He kept her locked in the present rather than the familiar, cold nightmare that would take over the moment she was alone again. He didn't ask questions and she was grateful. He set her on the bed. She sat on the edge, wrapped her arms around his waist and kept her face pressed against him.

"You didn't answer my calls," he said.

Emma didn't reply.

"I forgot our anniversary."

"It's fine," she muttered.

Peter cupped her chin and tilted her face up. He examined her for several beats.

"You look tired."

He didn't know the difference between her being devastated or tired. She would count that as a positive thing since it meant less questions.

"Are you okay? What happened?" Peter asked.

Emma didn't answer. She wouldn't tell Peter about her encounter with Ben or that her parents died on this date two years ago. That was her burden to bear and she wouldn't bother him with it. They didn't have that type of relationship anyway. Right now, she needed to know she wasn't alone. She pulled her sweater over her head and saw his eyes drift over her.

"You're not angry?" he asked carefully.

In response, she stood up and pulled off her jeans. She began to unbutton his shirt and he let her. When she was done, she dropped his shirt on the ground and raked her nails down his abdomen. One hand cupped the back of her head as their lips met. His hand skimmed over her flat tummy and squeezed her breast. Emma moaned into his mouth and Peter's lips curved. He pinned her to the bed and groaned at the feel of her naked beneath him.

She reached for the button on his slacks, but he pulled away and unzipped only enough for his cock to spring free. She arched to put him where she wanted, but he shifted, taunting her. Her nails scrabbled over his back.

"Peter, please," Emma moaned.

He slid into her and watched her eyes close and mouth drop open in pleasure. He loved the way she responded to him. She didn't hold anything back from him in bed. She gave herself completely and it was addicting. God, why had he stayed away from her for so long? He wouldn't last. Emma knew him too well. She pulled him down and bit his neck. He surged into her and she gasped. One hand fisted in her hair as he looked down at her.

"Do you want me?" he hissed.

She opened her eyes and gripped his sides. "Always."

Make me forget, she thought and he did.

~

*E*mma sat on the porch and sipped coffee as she watched the sun reflect off the lake below. The grass was wet with dew and birds chirped in a nearby tree. She woke wrapped in Peter's arms. She savored the moment before she got up, showered and made coffee. She still felt off kilter. The rollercoaster of emotions she experienced in the past two days left her numb.

Last night changed nothing for her. She knew she had to let him go. Their relationship wasn't what she wanted it to be —like Anna or Georgina's. She wanted her man to be there for her, to stand with her when times got rough. She and Peter had chemistry, but it didn't go deeper than that. Everyone in her town knew what happened two years ago. They knew the significance of this date and they gave her sympathetic looks and patted her on the back, but the man she slept with for a year had no idea… and he didn't want to know either. He wanted a willing, warm woman. He didn't want the sticky feelings or history.

She would rather be alone than be in a relationship that was only skin deep. She was grateful he was here, that he'd come to see her when he realized he forgot their date. That was uncharacteristically sensitive of him. There were several moments when he looked at her last night, almost as if he sensed there was something behind her urgency for him, but he didn't push. He gave her exactly what she needed— passion, comfort and rest. That was enough.

"Hey."

Emma got to her feet when she saw him standing

behind the screen door. He wore only his boxers. She pushed open the door and accepted the soft kiss he pressed on her lips. She hugged his warm body to her and rested her face against his chest for a moment. She couldn't help herself. Yearning filled her. A limbo relationship wasn't that bad, right? Then she remembered Georgina and Leo and tamped down her emotions. She deserved better and so did he.

Peter poured himself a cup of coffee and settled in the living room. She perched across from him on the arm of the love seat and he frowned.

"Thanks for coming to see me," she said.

"I'm sorry I forgot. It won't happen again," Peter said.

She pondered for a moment. She hadn't left a message so... "Tommy called you, didn't he?"

His face gave nothing away. "I can't say."

"Damn, Anna. She has a big mouth."

"You should have told me," he said, tone faintly reproving.

Emma sputtered into her coffee. "I called a week ago to remind you *and* I called the night of. Your phone was off."

"I screwed up bad, didn't I?"

"What's done is done."

Peter heard the distance in her voice. "I'll make it up to you."

"You don't need to make it up to me. It wasn't a big deal."

"It's our one-year anniversary. It is a big deal."

She braced herself and said every man's least favorite sentence. "We need to talk."

"Okay." When she was silent for a minute he bit out, "What's wrong with you?"

The hand holding the mug trembled ever so slightly. "Nothing."

He sensed he wasn't going to like this. When had Emma ever initiated a talk? Never. "I can tell you're not okay. I

45

forgot about you and I feel like shit. The date never crossed my mind."

Because it doesn't mean anything to you, she thought. "I think we should break up."

Peter jerked. "What did you say?"

"I think it's time. We've run our course."

"We've run our course," he repeated.

"We live in different cities and we both have businesses to run. We were bound to come to an end sooner or later."

Her heart sank when he didn't move, didn't speak. Was he relieved? Angry? She couldn't tell.

"Don't you think this is something we should talk about?" he asked finally.

She shook her head. "No. I was hoping we could stay friends."

"Friends?" The force of his voice was so explosive, she jumped. "Emma, you're going overboard here. You just said you're not angry and now you're breaking up with me? Don't you think you're overreacting?"

She gripped her hands together. "I'm not angry. I just realized we're not meant to be together. I was hoping we could part on good terms. I mean, we enjoy each other. We're friends."

"We're a hell of a lot more than friends! We've been lovers for a year! That's the longest relationship I've been in!" He rose and paced towards the window and back. "Jesus, I forget one thing and you're ready to break up with me. What the hell is wrong with you?"

"I haven't seen you for a month," she said defensively.

"I've been busy!" he spat, still pacing.

"This isn't the first time you've put business before me."

He jabbed a finger in her direction. "So that's what this is about. I own a huge company. I'm bound to miss a few things."

46

"Yes, you are. That's why I'm breaking this off."

Why was he making this harder than it needed to be? Shouldn't he just shrug and walk out? Isn't that what guys do? It's what Ben did. What was the matter with him? Maybe she was the first woman to break up with him and he didn't know how to handle it. Maybe that's why he wasn't taking this well.

"You're breaking up with me because I missed a couple of dinners?" he asked with such scorn, she flushed.

It was her turn to rise from her chair. He was turning it all on her, trying to make her feel like she was wrong when he was the one who couldn't keep his commitments. "I'm breaking up with you because this is bound to keep happening. Why are you fighting with me about this?"

"Why?" He came toe to toe with her. "Because you're overreacting."

She didn't back away. "Fine. I'm overreacting. You don't want to be with an irrational female. Goodbye."

Even as the words flew out of her mouth, she inwardly wrung her hands. This was turning out ten times worse than she imagined. Why were they yelling at each other? *Walk away*, she told her body, but it seemed drawn like a magnet to the man in front of her vibrating with fury.

"What's gotten into you?" Peter demanded.

She gave his chest a shove that made no impact on him whatsoever. "There's nothing wrong with me. It's you—" She stopped herself and shook her head. "There's no point in this. We both need to move on."

"Move on?"

"Yes. Move on. It's going to be a new year. We can both start off fresh."

"There must be more to what you're saying. You're just telling me out of the blue that we're over?"

"You care for me like you care for your car. When it has

trouble, you fix it. You like its convenience, but you forget about it most of the time because it'll be where you left it."

"I care," he insisted.

She sighed, "I think you do but—"

"But what?"

"I want someone who's here, someone who doesn't forget dinners and anniversaries. Someone present."

"I work in the city. You need to understand that."

"I do! That's why I'm breaking it off. I need someone here. You need someone more… understanding than me."

"You're not making sense," he muttered.

"You must have known this was coming."

"Do I look like I knew this was coming?" he shouted.

"Don't yell at me!" Her blue eyes speared him. "You think I haven't felt you holding back from me? I've been seeing you less and less. It's time for us to let this go."

"I want you in my life! Why do you think I keep coming back to you?"

"Sex."

"I can have sex any time I want," he said and froze.

He saw hurt flicker over her face, but she didn't break eye contact.

"I know you can."

He started towards her. "I didn't mean that."

She held up a hand and this time he stopped. "You're one of the most eligible bachelors in the city. You can have anyone you want. I don't know why you keep coming back to me, but sooner or later, you'll get tired of coming here. One of us has to end it."

His eyes narrowed. "I want you."

She shook her head. "You'll get over it."

He ran a hand through his hair. "Jesus, I come here because you're the only one that doesn't pressure me for anything. You're not asking me how much money I rake in, where our relationship is going or even when I'll be back. You just go with the flow."

"We don't even *sound* like a normal couple," she moaned.

"You mean something to me, you must know that."

You mean something to me, she thought. Emma remembered the way Leo watched Georgina, the way Tommy went out of his way for Anna. She thought of her parents and the way they doted on each other. It wasn't enough. She deserved more, right? She deserved someone who was crazy about her. She and Peter had chemistry, but they tiptoed around each other's emotions and were careful not to intrude over invisible boundaries. Anger and hurt swirled in her chest, making it hard to breathe. Couldn't he see what she was saying? She cared too much and he didn't care enough.

"You mean a lot to me too," she said in a hollow voice, "but our relationship isn't based on anything concrete. We see each other whenever your schedule allows and we've never gone further."

"Is that why you're calling us off? Because you haven't gotten a commitment from me?" Peter said angrily. "Okay, what do you want?"

I want you to love me, to be here because I need you! "I'm not asking for anything."

"So instead of telling me what you need, you break up with me? You're acting crazy."

"Peter, you know what I'm saying is true. We don't have that kind of relationship—" she began when he hauled her against him and covered her mouth with his.

She tried to push him away, but his tongue delved into her mouth and she was engulfed in desire. Her mind shrieked at her that this wasn't a good idea, that great sex wasn't enough, but her body didn't care. She was starved for touch. She would deal with the pain later. Peter boosted her up and pinned her to the wall. She wrapped one arm around his neck as he unbelted her robe. His hand slipped between her legs and she moaned.

"When did you decide to break up with me?" he growled.

"Peter," she gasped and wrapped one hand around his wrist.

"When?" he challenged.

Her eyes sparked with need and fury. "Yesterday."

"So, you already knew you were going to dump me when you took me to bed."

Their eyes locked as he positioned himself and slid into her. Emma caught her breath and clenched inner muscles. The tendons in his neck stood out and the hand gripping her ass clenched.

"You want me just as much as I want you," he breathed and rolled his hips.

She gasped and bit her lower lip. When she would have closed her eyes against him, he commanded her to keep them open. She obeyed helplessly. He slowly thrust in and out of her. When she let out an impatient sound, his eyes glinted and he took her hard and fast. When she climaxed, she raked her nails down his back. He arched against her and came. Peter lowered her until her feet touched the ground. She shook uncontrollably against him. She couldn't stop the way her hands clutched at him. They panted for breath and when he looked down at her, his eyes were narrowed and cold. He pulled out of her slowly, making her shiver.

She leaned against the wall for support and pulled the edges of her robe together. Although they'd just had each other, she felt a chill begin to invade her bones. Peter never looked at her like this before. It was a mixture of betrayal and loathing.

"You want us to be over, so be it," he said.

He walked upstairs. She trembled and wrapped her arms

around herself. She heard him rummaging around and a minute later, he reappeared. He shrugged into his dress shirt and fastened his slacks. He didn't look at her as he slammed the door on his way out. The brief gust of frigid air that burst into the house made her shiver. She was alone again. It was better this way, right?

CHAPTER 6

*A*nna walked into the bakery at three in the morning to find Emma pulling out her first batch of almond poppy seed muffins. Emma baked when she was upset. Anna's lips tightened, but she didn't comment as she shrugged out of her jacket and got her apron. As Anna arranged muffins on a tray, she glanced at the dark circles under Emma's eyes. Her friend's normally animated face was blank.

"What happened?" Anna asked quietly.

Emma shook her head, not ready to talk and kept moving around the kitchen. Anna let her stew for half an hour before she stepped into Emma's path and wrapped her arms around her.

"Are you okay?"

Emma nodded. "I'm fine."

"No, you're not. You broke up with him?"

Emma nodded.

"Do you want him back?"

Emma shook her head violently, though her eyes were filled with conflicting emotions. "We're better off apart."

Anna squeezed her hands. "Are you sure this has nothing to do with the anniversary of your parent's death?"

"I guess it has something to do with it, but you can hardly call what we have a relationship. He hardly remembers me!"

"How did he take it?"

Emma blushed and then paled. "He was angry, but in the end, he agreed."

Anna's eyes widened. "He agreed?"

Emma got back to work. Anna wanted to grill her, but she saw the hurt brewing beneath the surface. For the next hour, neither spoke as they moved around the kitchen in perfect harmony, baking the pastries for the day. They were both lost in troubled thoughts. When the last sheets were put in the oven, Emma set the timer and moved to the coffee pot. Anna sipped her coffee and leaned against the counter, waiting.

Emma sighed. "I saw Ben."

Anna spewed coffee over the floor. "What?! When? Where?"

"Yesterday. At the graveyard."

"What did he say? What did *you* say?" Anna demanded.

"He said he was sorry, that he didn't know what to do that night and he still loves me," Emma said tonelessly.

Anna set her mug aside and rubbed Emma's stiff back.

"We argued. I don't think I can forgive him. When I saw him, all I could hear was what he said to me that night and remember him walking away while I held my mom and begged him to help. And Peter... I love him, but he doesn't know what my favorite flower is or how I like my coffee." When Anna looked confused, Emma waved it aside. "I'll get over Peter."

"Why didn't you call me? Geez, Ben *and* Peter? I don't know why you even came into work," Anna said, shaking her head.

"I don't want to be at home right now."

Anna nodded, understanding softening her face. "Georgina will be keeping us busy with her wedding. Not only are we making her cake and desserts, we're also her bridesmaids. We have fittings and favors to make on top of running the bakery."

Emma was cheered by this information. Anything to keep her busy was better than going home and remembering the way Peter looked at her before he left. "Bring it on."

∾

*D*erek slammed Peter's office door open. Peter didn't look up from the computer. He continued to type as Derek stalked over and slammed his hands on the desk.

"Okay, I give up. This has to stop!" Derek declared. "You're working yourself to death. I'll drive you to Bellingham myself!"

Peter didn't react or look at his friend. He continued to scowl at the computer screen.

"I mean it, Peter. It's been a month since you saw the baker chick, you look like crap and you haven't said a word to anyone."

Derek waited for a response and received nothing. He walked to an outlet in the corner and unplugged the computer. Peter erupted from the chair, grabbed his friend by the shirt and hauled him close.

"This is what you wanted, isn't it? You want me in the city, working my life away so we can get richer. I'm doing it, so leave me alone," Peter hissed.

Peter released his friend and plugged the computer back in. Derek hitched himself on the corner of Peter's desk and examined him closely. He usually reserved his intuition and observations for business, but he was worried about his best friend. It was Peter's own fault for taking on so much work that Derek had time to hassle him. Peter's normally messy office was so neat, Derek suspected he was cleaning it when he had nothing to do. Peter's hair was rumpled as if he kept running his hands through it, his suit was wrinkled and his eyes were bloodshot from lack of sleep.

"What the hell happened to you?" Derek demanded.

No response.

"Did something happen between you and the baker chick?" Derek ventured uncomfortably.

Peter's eyes flicked to him and the anger there told Derek all he needed to know. He held his hands up.

"Hey, I'm your friend. I'm just trying to help."

"You can help by leaving me the hell alone," Peter growled.

"Is she pregnant or something?"

Peter jerked as if he'd been shot. He stared at Derek for a full minute before he shook his head.

"No. She didn't say so."

"Oh." Derek raked his mind for another possibility. "She cheat on you?"

Peter gave him a baleful look. "She dumped me."

Derek hooted with laughter and slapped the desk. "For who?"

Peter glared. "No one. I forgot her on our anniversary. She says she needs someone who lives in Bellingham, someone *present*."

"Does she know who you are?" Derek asked incredulously.

"She doesn't care who I am."

"Doesn't care?" Derek repeated skeptically. "All women care about money."

"She has her own money."

Peter's hand tightened into a fist. He'd been blind-sided when she said she wanted to break up. He knew she had a right to be angry with him, but to break up with him after loving him through the night seemed so… cold. Fury caused him to show her what she was giving up, but it was he who ached for her. He was haunted by that vulnerable look on her face as she watched him leave. She craved him, cared for him, yet broke up with him. Why? It didn't make sense.

Since leaving her, he was forced to admit he took her for granted. He assumed he could keep his distance from her and come back whenever he wanted. Emma never whined or demanded anything from him. He knew he was at fault for some things, but why hadn't she talked to him instead of ending it? Normally, breaking up was a bluff to get a guy's attention, to have him correct his actions, but Emma wasn't playing a game. She meant it. She slept with him, calmly told him they were over and hoped they could be friends. What bullshit.

Emma didn't fight to keep him—she let him go as if the past year hadn't meant anything to her. That stung. He couldn't figure out the undercurrents in her mood. He sensed something else was going on, but he was completely at sea as to what that could be. He wondered if her bakery was in trouble, but Tommy cleared that up. If it wasn't money, what would compel her to kick him out of her life and start over? He was missing something huge, but he couldn't put his finger on it.

"You're scaring me," Derek said bluntly.

Peter glanced at his friend. "I'm fine."

"You're not."

"I will be."

"Do you, uh, like, love her?" Derek coughed.

Peter stared at him for a long moment before he shrugged. "I don't know."

"But you want her?" Derek was on more stable ground now, basic concepts he understood.

Peter hesitated for the briefest second before he said, "Yes."

"Well, what are you doing moping in Seattle?"

"*She* broke up with *me*," Peter said sourly.

Derek raised his brows. "When have you ever taken no for an answer?"

Peter didn't want to admit how battered he felt by Emma's words and actions. He turned his chair and looked out of the floor to ceiling windows that lined his office. He tapped his fingers thoughtfully on the arm of the chair. Emma desired him, but pushed him away. It slapped at his pride. Yes, he forgot their anniversary and he only made it down to Bellingham once a month, but she accepted that until now. What changed?

"This is why I only have one-night stands. Seeing you like this is depressing." Derek dug in Peter's desk drawers for something to eat. He came up with a bag of Doritos. He ripped open the bag and crunched noisily.

"Do you remember their faces?" Peter asked.

Derek munched thoughtfully. "For the most part."

"You're a bastard."

"I'll never be anything else." Derek slid off the desk and headed towards the door. "I don't expect to see you until you've either worked her out of your system or come back with her."

"Come back with her?"

"If you manage to sweet talk her, you're going to have to give her more than you gave before. Did you ever ask her to move to the city?" Derek asked with his mouth full.

Peter raised his brows. "For someone who's never been in a relationship, you seem to know what I'm supposed to do next."

"Women are all the same. Weren't you invited to a wedding in Bellingham this weekend?" Derek asked with a shudder.

Peter nodded and glanced at the invitation. "I don't know the couple, but the bride's father is a client of ours. I like him."

"Me too. Maybe you can put in an appearance at the wedding and then find your baker chick. Maybe their bakery is making the cake for the reception," Ben suggested.

Peter's mind leapt into overdrive. "I'll call our client and find out if he knows who's handling the desserts."

Derek winked and left, leaving Peter with a lot to think about. Could he get her back? Did he want her? His mind was set. He would find out why she broke up with him, fix it and all would be well again.

CHAPTER 7

*E*mma turned on soothing instrumental music while she painstakingly created sugar orchids and roses for Georgina's wedding cake. It had been a long month filled with business, dress fittings, wedding gift shopping and an elaborate bachelorette party. Georgina was euphoric. Emma's mouth curved into a smile as she painted the edges of a flower. Anna had a cake emergency in Seattle and begged Emma to make the flowers for Georgina's cake. Emma didn't mind. She gladly abandoned her paperwork to begin making the sugar flowers.

As the sun began to set, Emma stepped back to survey her work. Georgina's cake was a beautiful six-tier masterpiece with pearls at the base of each tier. Roses and orchids spilled from the top of the cake and twined around it in a vine of flowers that looked so real, she knew everyone wouldn't believe they were edible. Strategically placed crystals winked at her. Emma flexed her cramped hands and was grimly satisfied.

"Wow."

Emma turned and saw Anna's husband, Tommy. He was

exotic looking with his Polynesian heritage. Emma wrapped an arm around his waist as he came up beside her. They both surveyed the wedding cake in silence for several minutes.

"You did good," Tommy said.

"I know," Emma sighed, exhausted.

Tommy laughed. "I came to pick up Anna for dinner."

"She hasn't come back from Seattle yet."

He looked irritated for a moment and then focused on her. "How are you doing?"

"Fine."

"I heard from Peter."

Emma tensed. "That's nice."

"I didn't tell him about the accident."

"Thanks."

Tommy folded his arms across his chest. "I think you should tell him."

"It doesn't matter now. We're not together."

"Maybe if you told him, he'd understand—"

Emma held up a hand. "Tommy, I love you, but I really don't want to talk about Peter. It's over."

Tommy opened his mouth, but the back door opened and Anna swept in. Relieved, Emma turned to her. Anna stopped dead when she caught sight of the cake. She covered her mouth with a hand and her eyes filled with tears.

"Oh my God," Anna said reverently.

Emma took a bow. "I know. Now, we just have to move it."

They all glanced at each other. It took them a half hour to get up the guts to move the monstrous cake and when the deed was done, Emma was officially ready to go home. Tommy and Anna tried to convince her to go to dinner with them, but she declined. She drove home, warmed up a frozen meal and managed a few bites before her stomach protested.

She sat at the table in her kitchen and buried her face in her hands as tears pricked her eyes.

It had been a month since she broke up with Peter and she was plagued with loneliness and grief. Nightmares of the night of the accident were relentless and the break up with Peter only added to her stress. She cringed every time she remembered the way he looked at her before he left. She knew she'd done the right thing, but why did she have to feel so empty?

~

*B*y the time they gathered in the church to walk down the aisle, Emma's had the headache from hell. Her face felt tight from forcing herself to smile. All she wanted to do was crawl into bed and pull the covers over her head. Georgina and the other bridesmaids from the city were so full of nervous, giddy energy that Emma felt drained.

"Okay?" Anna asked with her arm linked through Tommy's.

"Yup," Emma said a trifle too brightly and wrapped her hand around her escort's arm.

To avoid Anna's suspicious frown, Emma looked around and saw Georgina whisper something to her father. They laughed together and then gave Georgina a fatherly kiss on the forehead. Emma's breathing hitched alarmingly as she faced forward. She straightened her spine and pasted a smile on her face when she felt like crying.

The hand that held the bouquet trembled. Her escort patted her hand sympathetically as they walked down the aisle after Anna and Tommy who were so in tune with each other, even their steps were in sync. The faces of those sitting in the pews were blurry dots she didn't try to focus on. She felt a burst of humor when she saw Leo waiting impatiently at the altar, looking past her for his bride. As Emma fell into line with the bridesmaids, Anna clutched her arm.

"I didn't know she invited him," Anna hissed.

"Who?" Emma whispered over the sound of the organ playing.

"Ben."

Emma scanned the crowd. It was easy to spot him because he was the only one who hadn't turned in their seat to watch Georgina come down the aisle. Ben was dressed formally, as she once imagined he would look at their own wedding. Even across the distance, his green eyes were piercing. Anna cursed beneath her breath. The other bridesmaids from the city wrinkled their nose at Anna's language.

"I don't know what he's doing here," Anna snapped.

Emma swallowed. "It's Georgina's wedding. She can invite anyone she wants. We all grew up together."

Her control wavered. Sensing this, Anna clutched Emma's left hand. She refused to show Ben how much seeing him upset her. Maybe he was here for Georgina and he would leave her alone. She hadn't seen or heard from him since their encounter in the graveyard and she hoped he stayed away so she could keep her composure.

The ceremony passed by in a blur and before she realized it, she was being escorted outside to pose for pictures. She'd never felt less like pretending to be happy. Ben stood on the sidelines, watching her with an unreadable expression on his face. Even with all the bitterness and hurt between them, she knew he was envisioning what they planned for their wedding as well.

Pandemonium reined as well wishers rushed to congratulate the newlyweds and people hopped into cars to get to the reception. In the crush, Emma lost sight of Tommy and Anna and was so focused on avoiding Ben that she didn't sense the other danger until a hard hand clasped her own and pulled her through the crowd. Shock made her stumble and she stared at the dark figure beside her. She tried to pull away, but he was relentless.

Peter led her to his convertible, deposited her into the passenger seat and closed the door before she could open her mouth to protest. He got into the driver's side and without a word, followed the long line of cars to the reception hall. Emma couldn't look at him. His anger filled the air. The month they'd been apart hadn't dimmed his temper. What was he doing here?

"You look beautiful," he said quietly.

"Thanks," she said faintly. She'd be damned before she showed him how much she missed him.

"I assume Ben is the guy with green eyes that couldn't take his eyes off you?" Peter's voice held no inflection.

Emma jerked and glanced sideways at him. Peter showed no reaction except for the slight tightening of his hands on the wheel.

"Is he?" he pushed.

"We're not together, Peter. It's none of your business."

"That's debatable. Has he been bothering you?"

"No. He's keeping his distance like I asked him to and I'm going to tell you the same thing—"

"When did you tell him?" Peter demanded.

"The day before I broke up with you," Emma snapped. She didn't need this right now. She didn't need both of her exes hounding her when she felt as if she might shatter.

"So, he's the reason why you were so angry that you jumped my bones."

Emma opened her mouth to deny it, but he shot her a glance which had her sitting back, fuming. "You didn't seem to mind."

"I don't mind you taking me to bed. I mind being used."

"I didn't use you! I wanted you. I *needed* you!" Her voice

cracked and when he reached for her, she huddled against the door. "Don't."

He retracted his hand. "Emma, I don't understand."

"You don't have to. It's over."

He shot her a dark look. "You still want me."

"So? You had your revenge."

He manipulated her into wanting him and walked out before her body came down from its climax. He showed her in no uncertain terms how little she mattered to him.

"We need to talk."

"No. I have to go to this reception and smile and… What are you doing here? You weren't invited. Don't you dare ruin Georgina's day," Emma warned.

"From the look on her face when she saw me, I'd say I enhanced it," he said sardonically.

"You're an arrogant bastard. Leave me alone."

"We're not finished, Emma."

"Yes, we are."

They pulled up to the reception hall. Emma got out before he could get around to her door. When she tried to walk off without him, he caught up to her and wrapped an arm around her waist. Her body reacted to his nearness and she remembered the feel of his warm skin beneath her fingers and her mouth watered. As if sensing her weakness, he leaned down and brushed his lips over the side of her neck.

"Move away from me and I'll embarrass the hell out of you. Got it?"

"What do you think you're doing?" she hissed.

He tried to look innocent, but was far from pulling it off. "I thought you wanted us to be friends."

"I changed my mind!"

Men drooled over his car while the bridesmaids from the city stared at him, open-mouthed. He led her into the hall, his grip warning her not to make a scene. She smiled at several locals who watched them avidly. Despite her predicament, Emma paused to admire the reception hall. Tiny lights shone through sheer white and plum drapes like stars. Candles flickered everywhere and the aroma of roses was welcoming and seductive. There was a crowd around Georgina's cake. Emma was pleased to see several people bend over to smell the sugar flowers. Everyone mingled and talked as they looked for their assigned tables. Without pause, Peter led her to the head table where the wedding party sat. To her astonishment, Peter held out a hand to Georgina's father.

"Glad to see you could make it," Georgina's father said jovially.

"Wouldn't miss it," Peter replied.

As Georgina's father turned to greet someone else, Emma felt her heart drop when she saw Peter's name next to hers at the table. Emma glared at Peter.

"Georgina's father is a client of mine," he said.

Anna and Tommy appeared and Emma turned to them gratefully. Anna looked at Peter as if he was scum and Peter returned her gaze blandly. One of the bridesmaids from the city nearly trampled on Emma's feet in her haste to introduce herself to Peter. Tommy held his hands up when Anna and Emma advanced on him.

"What is he doing here?" Anna demanded.

Tommy backed away. "He never told me he was coming to the wedding. I have nothing to do with this."

"If he thinks he can just waltz back into your life, he can forget it," Anna snapped.

"Introducing Mr. and Mrs. Leo Peters!" the announcer said and everyone cheered and clapped.

The newlyweds made their way to the table. Georgina broke away from Leo to introduce herself to Peter who kissed her cheek and thanked her for allowing him a place at her table.

"I'm honored," Georgina cooed and fanned herself behind Peter's back.

Emma wanted to run out the door. When Peter held out her chair, she shot him a killing glance before she sat. He settled beside her and when his thigh brushed against hers, she turned her back on him and talked to Anna who sat on her other side. Georgina frowned, confused by her body language. Inwardly wanting to scream, Emma tried to keep the smile on her face so Georgina wouldn't know something was very wrong.

In contrast to Emma's tension, Peter chatted easily with everyone. Emma felt as brittle as glass. Anna leaned over every once in a while to shoot angry looks at Peter, which he ignored while Tommy shifted uneasily in his seat. Emma forced herself to eat so she didn't have to talk to anyone. The restraint it took to keep herself in check resulted in a blinding headache.

When everyone headed to the dance floor, Emma used the opportunity to get away from Peter who was distracted by one of the bridesmaids who hung on his every word. Locals and classmates, she hadn't seen in years came up to hug and catch up. She began to relax and actually found herself relaxing a bit as she danced and teased Sam Belissimo. She turned away from him and came face to face with Ben.

They stared at one another while the dance music played and the voices around them faded. Ben reached out a hand, eyes steady and pleading. Ben had been her best friend and confidant and now… For a moment, she was tempted to place her hand in his. Once upon a time they'd been lovers and she believed they were soul mates. Seeing their classmates and most of the town dancing and laughing tonight made her yearn for the good old days where life had been simple and she knew where her life was headed. Ben knew her inside and out and she thought she knew him too, but... It hurt her to turn away from him, but she did it and bumped into Peter.

Before she could back away, Peter wrapped an arm around her and began to dance. She looked up and saw that his eyes were fixed over her shoulder on Ben.

"There's a lot you haven't told me," Peter observed.

Emma tried to draw back, but Peter tightened his hold. He never looked down at her as he navigated his way through the other dancers. She couldn't figure out what he was doing here, unless he wanted to throw it in her face how he was doing fine without her. She could see for herself that he was as handsome and untouchable as ever. When the song ended, Emma jerked away and left him standing on the dance floor.

CHAPTER 8

*E*mma stood outside with most of the wedding guests and waved while Georgina and Leo took off in their limo. Emma had never been more relieved to see a party end. She turned to Anna.

"Get me out of here."

Anna opened her mouth to reply, but Peter beat her to it.

"I'll take you home."

"No," Emma said without looking at him.

Anna bristled. "You've been gone for a month. If she meant so much to you—"

"He won't leave until they have it out, Anna," Tommy interjected.

"He's right," Peter agreed.

Anna put her hands on her hips, face reddening with anger. Emma knew she was about to blast Peter to bits with her Irish temper. Emma sighed and wrapped her arms around her friend so she wouldn't cause a scene.

"I can handle him," she whispered in Anna's ear.

"You don't have to."

"Yeah, I do. I'll see you later."

Emma stalked to Peter's car. When he opened the door for her, she got in, leaned back against the headrest and closed her eyes. He didn't try to talk on the drive to her house. He parked in her driveway and when he turned off the car and got out, her heart sank. She didn't have the energy to fight him. She was just so damn tired. She stopped in front of her door and turned to face him.

"Whatever you have to say to me, just say it," she said.

"Let's go inside."

"No."

Thoughts of their last encounter colored her cheeks. If he made a move, she wasn't sure she had the discipline to resist and he knew it. She remembered the disgust on his face the last time he left and shivered.

He leaned forward, dark eyes intense. "You don't want your neighbors to hear what I have to say to you."

He was a stubborn jerk. She unlocked the door and tossed her things on the table before she plopped on the couch. He remained standing. She clutched her hands together in her lap and waited.

"Are you pregnant?"

Emma's mouth dropped open. "What?"

"Are you?"

"No. Why?" she asked, totally bewildered.

"You lost weight and I heard you tell Anna you don't feel well. I figure that if you were pregnant and I missed our anniversary, that would make you dump me."

Emma noticed how tense he was. "No, I'm not pregnant."

"If you were pregnant, you would tell me, right?"

Emma hesitated for a second. "Yes."

"Good." He took a deep breath. "I've done a lot of thinking over the past month. I apologize for the way I reacted when you broke up with me. I wasn't thinking straight."

Emma stared at him. She hadn't expected this. Peter was so proud, so sure of himself. Right now, he looked uncomfortable and ill at ease.

"You're right. I took you for granted and I held back. The more attached I became to you, the more determined I was to show you how much I didn't need you."

She crossed her arms over her chest and said nothing.

"I forgot about our anniversary. I've rescheduled other dates and you never got angry, so I assumed you wouldn't mind this time either. I know I took you for granted, but I need to know why you broke up with me."

"I told you."

"No, you told me you needed someone present, that I didn't care enough. I care about you, a lot. I can be here more often. I'll make the time."

Emma yearned for him. A part of her wanted to let him hold her, but she knew it was only a temporary fix. He wanted her and 'cared' for her, but that wasn't a relationship. He wanted her on the sidelines, where he was comfortable with her, but it would never go beyond that.

"Does Ben have anything to do with this?" he persisted.

"Ben walked away from me when I really needed him. I thought we had a great relationship and it blew up in my face. I don't want to go through that again."

"Why'd he walk away?"

"He couldn't support me when my parents died. My parents loved each other. Everyone around them could feel it. This house is filled with it. I see it in Anna and Tommy and Georgina and Leo. I want that. I *need* that."

"You want love," Peter said without inflection.

She narrowed burning eyes on him. "I want someone who adores me, someone who will be there for me when it gets rough. Who *cares*. I don't want to be in a convenient relationship that leads nowhere."

"Why did you stay with me so long, then?" he probed.

"I thought…" she stopped and shook her head. "It doesn't matter."

"You love me?"

Anger and despair shot through her. He wouldn't stop until he'd taken everything from her. She didn't answer.

He spread his hands wide. "I've trampled on my pride to ask you for another chance. You think I like having you look at me as if you wish I'd leave? All night you pulled away from me like I was a stranger. The least you could do is give me the truth. You owe me that much."

"Owe you?" she choked and got to her feet. "We don't owe each other anything. We're done."

Peter grabbed her face and kissed her. She expected him to be rough and angry, as he'd been before, but the gentleness —the way his hand brushed over her cheek broke her. He kissed her lightly on the lips and brushed kisses over the tears she couldn't hold back any longer.

"It's not finished if you cry for me," Peter said hoarsely. "You love me, so you break up with me?"

"I don't want this," she said angrily and tried to pull away.

"You want me so much that you cry and push me away? I don't understand you at all. What do you want?"

"I told you!"

"You want a man here in Bellingham," he said scornfully. "You don't want anyone from this town. You want me and I want you."

She pulled away and was surprised when he let her go. She wanted to lose herself in him, wanted him so much, her body shook with need but her heart had too many punctures for her to go blindly.

"I love you," she whispered, tears coursing silently down her cheeks. "Do you love me?"

God, this was the hardest question she ever asked anyone.

Peter stared at her for several minutes. The sound of the clock ticking was the only sound in the room.

"I don't know," he said finally.

Emma wiped the tears from her face. "I'd rather live without love then be so close to it and not have it returned."

"What are you saying?"

"I'm saying you and I are done. I can't take the risk."

His face hardened and for a moment she thought it was going to be a replay of the last time he left. She tensed, but he walked to the door and closed it behind him. She listened to the sound of his BMW roar as it backed out of her drive. Emma let out a mewling sob and sank to her knees. She asked him the scariest question in the world and received her answer. There was no maybe in love. She was better off alone.

∼

"What are you doing here?" Anna snapped

She walked into her kitchen and glared at Peter who sat at the table with Tommy. She had to admit, Peter actually looked human for once. Peter eyed her balefully and took a long pull from his beer.

"Leave him be," Tommy told his wife.

Anna crossed her arms over her chest. "How's Emma?"

"By herself, the way she likes it," Peter rasped.

Anna was taken aback. "So, she managed to push you away."

Anna settled on the seat beside Peter and ignored the way he pushed his chair away from her.

"If you want to make snide remarks, I'll leave," Peter said.

Anna drummed her fingers on the table. Peter nursed his beer, trying to drown his emotions, which rocketed around in him.

"She didn't tell him," Tommy said to his wife.

Anna gave him a reproachful look. "It's her business."

"Look at him," Tommy protested. "She's killing him."

"Shut up, Tommy," Peter growled.

His gaze fell on a picture on the wall. He rose to get a better look. Emma, her parents, Ben and Anna beamed at the photographer. This was a version of Emma he'd never seen before. The joy on her face kept his eyes riveted on her. Emma wasn't a melancholy person, but he realized he'd never seen that particular sparkle in her eyes, never seen that smile on her face. His skin prickled.

"How old is this picture?" Peter asked.

The silence behind him was thick. He turned and looked at Anna.

"How long?" he demanded.

"It's two years old," Anna said.

"How did her parents die?"

There was a long silence while the married couple communicated with their eyes. Peter waited impatiently.

"In a car accident," Anna said slowly.

Peter glanced at the picture. "Ben knew her parents well."

Another silence.

"He was in the car when they died," Tommy blurted.

Peter wheeled around. "What?"

"Emma was driving," Anna said, eyes fixed on him. "They went around a curve and a car was stopped in the middle of the road. Emma slammed on the brakes too late. They were rear-ended. Her father died instantly and her mom..." Anna took a swig of Peter's beer and continued, "Their car was sandwiched between both cars. Emma's mom didn't have her seat belt on. She flew out of the car. Emma was hysterical."

Tommy rubbed Anna's back as she clasped her hands around the beer bottle.

"Ben couldn't handle what was happening. He walked

away and left Emma to deal with the carnage. Ben and Emma were the only survivors. Emma's mom died in her arms."

"The anniversary of her parent's death is the same week as your one-year anniversary. Emma and Ben were engaged back then," Tommy said in a rush.

"Engaged?" Peter repeated, stunned.

"Emma and Ben have been together for as long as I can remember. After the accident, Emma couldn't even look at him. He moved away and he's never visited until now. I can't imagine how Emma feels when she sees him," Anna said.

Peter remembered the look on Emma's face when she came home and jumped into his arms. Her eyes were glassy and she'd been pale as milk. He knew something was wrong, but he expected her to tell him. She hadn't. She held onto him so tightly and he didn't have a clue what she was going through. Everything suddenly made sense. Why keep so much from him when she loved him? The answer came to him quickly. Peter wanted to bang his head against the wall. When had he ever shown her that he cared?

"Since the accident, Emma tries not to care for others because she loves so deeply. She expects people to walk away from her just like you did. She doesn't ask people to stay— she lets them go so she has time to pull back before going too deep. I don't think she even realizes she's doing it."

Peter couldn't stop the blast of fury. "I butchered my pride to go back to her!"

Anna was unfazed. "Good for you. I guess the real question is, how much do you want her?"

CHAPTER 9

a week later, Emma drove out of Bellingham. She needed time to regroup and relax. When Emma reached Seattle, she checked into a hotel and found comfort in the faceless people who didn't know or care about her. She checked on the bakery, which was doing exceptionally well. She stayed in the back office, examining and adjusting the finances and made time for the employees who needed to talk to her about ideas, vacation and peak times when they would need to hire more staff. Emma received a call from Anna around noon.

"How's everything there?" Anna asked.

"Good. Everything's in order."

"Good. You're on the eight o'clock ferry tomorrow, right?"

"Yeah, call me if you need me."

"I will," Anna promised. "Take care."

After Emma closed the bakery, she strolled along the waterfront while a breeze tugged on the ends of her scarf. The sea rocked moodily and she wandered aimlessly, forcing herself out of business mode and into a slower gear.

Tomorrow she would ride the ferry to Victoria, British Columbia where she and her parents vacationed in the summers. She looked up at the towering buildings and wondered which one Peter worked in and if he ever wandered the streets of Seattle. She doubted it. Emma stopped when she felt the first rain drop splash on her forehead.

"*So* Seattle," she muttered.

She took refuge in the nearest restaurant, which turned out to be a warm cafe that served great coffee and sandwiches. She sat at a table near the front windows and watched the rain pour down. Tourists scurried while natives pulled tiny umbrellas out of pockets and purses, creating colorful mushrooms everywhere. She ordered a sandwich, soup and tea and nibbled while she let her thoughts drift. It was nice not to have an agenda. She had a month to recoup, exorcise Peter from her heart and put her life into perspective.

"Mind if I join you?"

Emma's head jerked up. She stared nonplussed at Peter who stood in front of her in a black trench coat, hair wet from the rain. Their eyes met and her heart melted and tore. Love, regret and sorrow scraped along her nerves. Her body flooded with heat. Would she be able to see him in the future and not want him?

"What are you doing here?" she asked.

He settled into the chair across from her. Their knees bumped beneath the small table and she jerked back.

He ignored her reaction and said, "I heard you were in the city."

"Heard?" she repeated. "I need to talk to Tommy about gossiping."

"We're friends, aren't we? It was natural for him to mention you'd be here."

"Peter." She didn't know what to say. Seeing him again brought back all the yearning she didn't want to feel. She was going on vacation to get over him, not to wonder why she let him go. "I can't do this."

"I'm not going to pressure you about anything. I just wanted to see you."

She cocked her head to the side. The anger he displayed at the wedding was gone as if it had never been. She remembered the anger on his face when she told him she wouldn't take a chance on him. What changed since then?

He raised a brow. "I want to try to be friends."

"Friends?" she parroted. This was the last thing she expected from him.

Heat lit his eyes and her body tingled in reaction.

"I want you, but as you're so dead set against us being together, I'll settle for being friendly."

"You're losing your mind," she observed.

"My business partner, Derek, thinks so," Peter said with a shrug and stole one of her French fries. "My place isn't far from here. Want to see it?"

She couldn't stop the small spurt of curiosity, but she didn't want to encourage his bizarre behavior. He was in a strange mood. He wasn't angry, he wasn't happy, he was… placid. It was so unlike him. Like any workaholic, Peter filled every moment of his day with things to do. Roaming the city to see a "friend" was definitely out of character.

"I don't think that's a good idea," Emma said.

"You're probably right," he said philosophically. "How's the bakery doing?"

"Better than expected."

"Whenever there's an event at the office, we get our cakes from there."

Peter didn't ask before he took a bite from the other half of her sandwich.

"Oh," Emma said, surprised and touched. She knew his influence gave their small bakery much needed advertisement. "Thanks."

"It's good," Peter said with a shrug.

Emma was at a loss for words, so she looked back at the rainy city. She clasped her hands beneath the table to stop herself from reaching for him.

"You're here alone?" Peter asked, finishing off her sandwich.

"Yes."

"Have you seen Ben since the wedding?"

The question snapped her out of her internal struggle and she refocused. Did she detect an edge in his tone? "No, I haven't seen him. He knows when I say to leave me alone, I mean it."

The look Peter shot her was that of a dominant male. "It depends on the man."

"I guess it depends on their history," Emma said.

"Care to elaborate?"

Emma looked away. "No."

The tension between them made her shift in her seat. Things left unsaid between them crackled in the silence. Peter finished off her meal and paid the bill. She didn't fight him, she knew better. By the time they left, the rain turned into a light mist. Peter produced a basic black umbrella. It flared above him and he stood on the sidewalk while raindrops dripped sullenly around him. His eyes were hooded and broody as he waited for her to come to him. When she did, she sensed him relax slightly.

"What do you think of the city?" he asked.

Glad for the neutral subject, she said, "I don't mind Seattle, but I like having my own house, seeing the lake and being in a small town. You love the city, don't you?"

"I like the convenience the city offers, but I think I've started to outgrow it a bit."

"You're moving?"

He shrugged. "Not sure if it should be a bigger city or a small town."

"You should slow down," Emma said without thinking. "You need to learn how to balance your life."

"You're one to talk. Is that why you're going on vacation?"

She looked up to find him watching her closely. He was too damn close. Pedestrians forced her into closer proximity to him and she could smell his cologne. "I need time to myself."

"We all need that."

She snorted. "I don't think you've ever been on vacation."

"I was on vacation when I met you."

"You spent two weeks turning up everywhere I went and bullied me into going on a date. Even that *vacation*, you turned into a mission."

In spite of everything, she felt her heart lift a little. He'd been a welcome distraction. He didn't give her a chance to grieve her parents that September.

"Once I got you, I enjoyed my vacation." Emma rolled her eyes and he continued, "At eighteen, I charted my path. I knew exactly what I wanted, who I wanted to be and how to get there. I never looked back."

"You knew what you wanted at eighteen?" Emma thought back to that age. "Anna wanted to be a pastry chef. I didn't know what I wanted to be so I went to culinary school with her. My heart wasn't in it so I decided to do the business side. It's worked out well."

Peter nodded. "Thinking of expanding?"

"I think one in town and one in the city is good enough for now. We're making a good profit and we want to be in control of it, so what we have is fine."

They walked into the hotel and up to her room. She turned to him after she opened the door, half expecting him to barge in. He didn't. They stared at one another for a long minute.

"If you need anything, call me," he said and closed the door for her.

Emma looked out the peephole and didn't see a thing. Was Peter playing with her or did he really want to be friends? She stood there for several minutes, sure that he wouldn't go out of his way to find her and then leave, but she realized he'd done just that. What was he up to?

$\approx$

*E*mma leaned against the rail of the ferry and breathed in the chilly air. *I need this break*, she thought. From work, from men and from Anna's fussing. People had to move on after loved ones died. She knew that. She put one foot in front of the other and appeared to be recovered from the loss, but she was far from it. She was as much of a workaholic as Peter. She grimaced at the thought. She spent more time at work than she did anywhere else. After the accident, she tried to take a leaf out of her mother's book and stopped trying to plan her life, which is how she ended up with Peter. Well, she was going to Victoria so she could relax and figure out what her next step should be.

Someone came up beside her and leaned on the rail. They were a bit too close for comfort. She sidled sideways and when the person moved just as smoothly, she looked up and her mouth sagged open. Peter stared out at the ocean and didn't react to the low growl she released.

"What the hell are you doing here?" she demanded.

"I thought I'd take a vacation," he said easily.

"Then get your own damn ferry!"

"You knew this wasn't over between us."

So that's why he didn't push her yesterday. "You said you just wanted to see me. Now you're stalking me?"

He looked offended. "I'm not stalking you, I'm *escorting* you."

"I don't need an escort. And since when do you take vacations?"

"Since my business partner told me to leave until I become human again." He leaned towards her. "Give it up. I'm coming with you."

"I want to be alone."

"No, you don't. We both have time off and we can figure out what we want."

"I already know what I want—to be alone!"

"Just think of it as a concerned friend keeping you company."

"I thought we had this conversation last night. We've never been just friends."

"It's never too late to start."

She put her hands on hips. "I don't know who you think you are—"

"Just shut up, Emma."

She slapped her hands on the metal railing. "You realize I've seen you more in the past two months than I normally would in six?"

He ignored her. "I've been thinking I need to revise the plan I made when I was eighteen."

She blinked. "Why? You have exactly what you want."

"Exactly. I need new goals."

She stared at him as if he'd grown two heads. "That's great that you want to find yourself, but I want a relaxing vacation and that doesn't include you!" She could see her peaceful vacation going up in smoke.

He held up a hand like a boy scout. "I swear I'll be good."

"That's great. Go somewhere else."

"Just do whatever you planned in Victoria. I'll tag along."

There was no reasoning with him. Although she kept up a steady stream of objections and complaints on the three-hour ride to Victoria, he didn't rise to the bait and remained freakishly even-tempered. When they reached Victoria, there was a man waiting with a SUV for Peter. When the man handed the keys over, Emma tried to escape. Peter grabbed the back of her jacket and hauled her back.

"Emma, don't. The car's here. You don't need to rent your own."

He talked to her as if she were a child. Her cheeks flushed with temper.

"You aren't staying with me at the cottage."

"Yes, I am."

She puffed up like an angry owl. "This is *my* vacation. You have another thing coming if you think I'm going to let you intrude on my hideaway. I need time to rest, not cater to anyone, least of all *you*."

He didn't react to her tirade. He leaned against the car and waited for her to run down. The men that passed stared at Peter as if he were insane to let a woman talk to him that way. The women gave Emma a thumbs up behind his back or covered their mouths to muffle their laughter.

"I know you don't want me here," Peter interjected when she paused to catch her breath. "I know you think I don't care about you, but I do. I won't pressure you for anything. We have unfinished business and I think we need to spend time together."

She stomped her foot like a child. "Are you listening to me?! We're over. You had your chance! We need to move on!"

"Fine. You broke up with me, but we're still going to see each other when I visit Tommy. I'll be damned if you ice me the way you do Ben."

Emma took a step back as if he slapped her. Why did he keep bringing up Ben? He was such a sore subject that just the mention of him made her stomach churn.

"You have no idea what happened between Ben and I!"

"Maybe you should enlighten me. All I know is, you two have a past and he still loves you."

She felt cornered and harassed. "If you knew—"

He waited expectantly, but she didn't say anything more. As if he could tell he pushed her too far, he wrapped his arms around her. Peter wasn't the touchy type, especially in public. It startled her into looking up at him.

"Give me time, Emma, for both of us."

She looked at Peter, *really* looked at him. Something was different. He wasn't Peter Logan the successful businessman or Peter the sensational lover. He was himself, as she'd never seen him before. He wore jeans, a shirt and tennis shoes. He seemed at ease, which was so unlike him. She eyed him suspiciously. She didn't buy his offer of friendship, but it was obvious he wasn't going anywhere. She was bound to run into Peter in Bellingham since their best friends were married. It was inevitable...On the flip side, being the workaholic Peter was, he would freak out within a few days and hurry back to Seattle to take care of his precious business so she wouldn't have to endure this for long.

"I don't think this is a good idea," she muttered.

"We won't know unless we try."

She threw up her hands. "We've been *trying* for a year!"

"Maybe we didn't make it as a couple, but we can be friends."

"I'm not planning on leaving the cabin at all. I'm going to do my nails, read and draw."

"I brought my laptop. That's all I need."

"You're coming no matter what I say, aren't you?"

"Yup."

"What if this doesn't work?" she asked, arms crossed.

"At least we tried."

Wondering if she was losing her mind, she got into the SUV and slammed the door. Peter was smart enough not to smirk when he got into the driver's seat. When she opened her mouth to give directions, Peter pulled out a GPS that already had the address of her parent's cottage. She narrowed her eyes at him.

"You're so damn sure of yourself," she accused.

"More like I needed the address in case you managed to ditch me somehow."

"How much time do you have off?" Emma asked.

"As long as I want. Derek's taking care of everything."

Peter drove through Victoria, which was beautiful in autumn. It was a beautiful day with sunlight bouncing off the water. Emma secretly bet Peter wouldn't last longer than three days in a cottage with no activities or stores within an hour's drive. Despite Peter's presence, she felt her spirits lift. She had good memories here. She hadn't been back since her parent's passed.

"I've never been here before," Peter said.

"It's my home away from home."

"I can see why."

As they approached the cabin, she leaned forward, desperate for that first glimpse of home. When she saw the cabin, nestled in a shelter of trees towering high above, she clapped her hands together. As soon as the SUV stopped, Emma jumped out. She rushed towards a wood chip path that led to the back of the house. The cottage perched on the edge of a cliff with the sea stretching out as far as the eye could see. A chilly wind whipped through her hair and sent it streaming backwards like a banner. She closed her eyes and took a deep breath.

"It's beautiful," Peter murmured behind her.

"There's a path that leads down to a pebble beach," Emma said, pointing to a steep path.

"You own the cabin?"

She nodded. "We used to come here during the summer. This is a peaceful place. I want it to stay that way."

She glanced at him and saw him nod. He admired the view in silence. She hoped he understood that this was a special place to her. The spirits of her parents rested here.

They stood in silence for several minutes before they went to get the bags. The cabin had two bedrooms with an airy kitchen, fireplace and huge living room. It was well-maintained and happy memories of her childhood flooded back. When she set her bags down in one of the rooms, she picked up a sketch her mom did of Emma and her dad. Emma set the sketch down as her throat locked and collapsed face down on the bed.

She was in an isolated cabin with her ex. Why? Because no wasn't in his vocabulary. She could hear him moving around in the next room and she groaned into the mattress. This was supposed to be a vacation where she could center herself and go back to a life without a man. Why couldn't Peter understand that she didn't want to take a chance on someone who didn't know if he loved her or not?

"Emma?"

She groaned and turned her head to the side. Peter leaned against the doorjamb with his arms crossed.

"What?" If he said this place was a dump, she would kill him.

"There's no food in the house."

"I know. I haven't been here for years."

"Let's go, then."

She got up and jabbed a finger at him. "This is a *vacation*. This isn't the city where we have to do everything right at this moment."

"I'm hungry."

She snorted. "I can see why we need groceries. Okay, let's go."

∾

*E*mma followed Peter into the store. He casually pushed a purple shopping cart as if he did this every day, which couldn't be further from the truth. If any of his colleagues in Seattle could see him now, they'd keel over in shock. Peter spent a lot of time in the cereal aisle and seemed to know a great deal about the different type of meats, which surprised Emma.

"I can cook. I just don't need to," he said when she stared at him.

"You've never cooked for me," Emma said with her hands on hips.

"I'm rusty. But, since I'm inviting myself on your vacation, I'll cook as long as we're here."

Emma perked up. "Really? Like what?"

"Well, I can make lasagna tonight, we can have meatloaf another night. What else?"

Emma had a sudden mental image of him wearing nothing but a white chef apron in the cabin kitchen. She waved a hand to dismiss the image. "Whatever you want to make is fine."

"Where's the wine aisle?"

∾

*A*fter a surprisingly delicious meal, Emma sat on the back-porch swing, watching the sunset. She lifted the glass to her lips and let the wine warm her. Peter came out on the porch with his own glass and settled beside her.

They touched from shoulder to knee. He didn't comment as they watched color streak the sky.

"It was really good," Emma said for the fifth time.

"I'm glad you liked it. It feels good doing normal stuff. I can't remember the last time I went to a grocery store or cooked."

She tapped her fingernails on the wine glass. "Is this the way you pictured your life when you were eighteen?"

Peter began to push the swing with the toe of his shoe. "Yes, but I didn't think of the price I had to pay to be rich."

She glanced at him. "That's the goal you set? To be rich?"

"I wanted to be independent, to have my own money so I wouldn't depend on anyone."

She nodded and her mind conjured up Ben. When he deserted her at the accident, she realized how much she depended on him because for a minute she had been paralyzed with shock, disbelief and fear, but she got the job done. She was wary of depending on anyone again, especially a man who was so strong-willed. Peter didn't need anything from her, from anyone. She knew him well enough to know that Peter needed freedom. She needed too much. He didn't have it in him to give her what she craved—love, a family, a home.

"There's a lot of sketches everywhere," Peter said, breaking into her thoughts.

"My mom was an artist," Emma said and realized this may be the first time she ever mentioned talked about her parents.

"She was talented."

Emma nodded. "It was the one thing my mom and I had in common."

"You're not like your mom?"

Plied by wine and food, Emma relaxed despite Peter's presence. "No. My mom was a free spirit. I'm organized like my dad. I was always working and I liked it that way. When we came here, my mom wouldn't let me work. We drew, hiked and had fun."

Her voice trailed off and Peter glanced at her.

"I'm sorry about your parents."

She cleared her throat. "I'm gonna turn in."

Emma rose, retreated to her room and closed the door. She reached for the phone to call Anna and demand to know what part her friend had in Peter crashing her vacation, but stopped herself. She was an adult. She could handle Peter.

CHAPTER 10

$\mathcal{E}$mma tiptoed over the wooden floor when she actually felt like stomping. She hadn't slept well. Peter's voice carried from the living room to her bedroom as he took care of business. She heard snippets of conversation as she faded in and out of sleep. His voice slipped into her dreams and she woke wanting him. She pummeled her pillow to get rid of excess energy. Being around Peter and trying to maintain that emotional distance felt strange. She still loved him. How the hell could she get over someone she was living with for the foreseeable future?

The sun wasn't up, but she didn't care. She needed air. She poured coffee into a travel mug and added a liberal amount of cream. She saw uncomfortable reminders of Peter scattered around. It made her feel strange. Even though they dated for a year, he never stayed with her for long, so his belongings were always in a neat pile. Now, his watch, laptop and papers lay on the table. It looked like he was settling in.

She exited the cabin and lugged an old blanket, her mug and sketchpad. She flipped on the porch light and settled on the swing. She wrapped herself in the blanket and listened to the sea. She sipped coffee to warm her and let her mind settle. She forced all problems, worries and desires to the side and focused on her heart like her mom taught her. Drawing was about expressing yourself. There didn't have to be a goal or a plan. It didn't even have to make sense. Art just… was. She flipped to a blank page in the sketchpad and spun a pencil between her fingers for a moment before she began.

Emma was rational and analytical by nature, a contrast to her mom who was a romantic artist. Her mom worried that Emma spent too much time on business and less on enjoying life. Emma and her mom were opposites in most things, but they both drew from the heart. Drawing bared Emma's soul and showed her vulnerabilities. Even before the death of her parents, she hated the feeling of being exposed when someone looked at her work because it came from a private part of her that dreamed and needed.

Emma didn't draw the scene around her, she drew snapshots of memory. She felt compelled to draw the images she dreamt about. Usually, the only time she drew nowadays was for cake designs, but right now there was no agenda. It was just her, the blank page and her memories. The scratch of the pencil and the sound of the sea beat back the outside world. She examined the scene taking place on the page, rocked the swing for a minute and continued.

Before the sun rose, Emma stared down at a rough sketch of Peter in Seattle standing on the sidewalk with his umbrella flared out, rain pouring down around him. He looked every inch the tycoon with his business suit and well-cut trench coat. His eyes bored into hers, intent and challenging. She didn't examine the picture too closely. She flipped the page and her pencil began to move of its own accord. She lost herself in the strokes, the lines and shading as she tried to make each memory come to life.

"Emma?"

She raised the pencil and blinked. The sun was up and Peter stood beside the swing. He looked down at the sketch with an unreadable expression on his face.

"Breakfast is ready," he said.

"Breakfast?" Emma rose from the swing, wincing as her body cramped.

"How long have you been out here?"

"I have no idea." Emma hobbled into the house and her mouth watered at the smell of bacon. "How long have you been up?"

"About an hour. How'd you sleep?"

She didn't look at him as she answered, "Fine."

The table was set with eggs, bacon and fruit.

"Wow."

"I told you I'd feed you while I'm here."

"So, you did."

Emma felt no shame in taking more than her share of food. Drawing was therapy for her and she already felt better. She didn't feel as tense and the sexual hunger that kept her up through the night was muted. She was halfway through the tasty breakfast when she realized Peter wasn't eating. His eyes were fixed on the sketchpad, which was flipped open to a sketch of Ben in the graveyard. That devastated look on Ben's face when she walked away from him that day ripped at her soul. Love, anger, understanding and loss filled Ben's eyes. She knew every line of Ben's face even after all this time and it made her ache for what had once been between them. Having Peter witness such a personal memory made her skin itch. The insecure part of her wanted to snap the book shut, but the woman in her refused. She had nothing to hide.

"You loved him a lot, didn't you?" Peter's voice was very low.

Inwardly, she flinched. *This is why I don't like showing my work to people*, she thought. When Emma drew, she let go of the rational part of her mind and just *felt*. If she was honest with herself and let her heart lead, the emotion she invested into each picture translated clearly.

"I did," she said.

"You don't love him anymore?"

The hand holding her coffee cup trembled and she set it down firmly. "I love him, but there's other emotions mixed in that overpower love."

His hand hovered over the sketchpad. "May I?"

Emma hesitated. Even when her silence became uncomfortable, Peter didn't back down. She finally gave her consent with a shrug. He opened the book and flipped through four sketches. He spent a long time on each page, even flipping back and forth between scenes, probably trying to figure out what the common thread was. There was a storyline to the images, but they were out of order.

Peter's face was unreadable, which made her fingers tighten around her fork. Seeing Peter handle her work was like handing over the most secret part of herself and asking for approval and understanding. She chastised herself for being so sensitive, but this was Peter. She didn't want him to understand her art because it would give him another facet of herself when she was trying to pull away. She jiggled her foot anxiously beneath the table where he couldn't see.

She finished off the last of her food, but Peter wasn't finished examining her work. Nerves screaming, she took her plate to the sink, washed the dishes and wiped down the stove. Still, he sat quietly. When she couldn't take it anymore, she went over to him and held out a hand.

"Can I have it back?" she asked.

Peter's finger brushed over a sketch of Emma's parents. They sat on the floor in front of a fire. Her father had his arms wrapped around her mother who leaned back against him. They both stared into the flames. The love between the couple was unmistakable.

Peter looked up at her and butterflies erupted in her stomach.

"You're very talented," he said in a subdued tone.

"Thanks."

She tried to snatch the sketchpad, but he moved it out of her reach.

"You have a hard time trusting people, don't you?"

Emma froze. "What makes you say that?"

"I was with you for a year and not once did you mention you're an artist."

"I'm not an artist. I'm a businesswoman." She was off balance and hating it.

"You hide behind business and numbers, but you show what you really value when you draw." He held up the picture of her parents and her heart tore. "I can feel how much you miss them."

She hadn't expected him to read anything beyond the obvious in her art. He watched her steadily, waiting for her to say something, but she didn't know what he wanted from her. He turned to the sketch of himself in Seattle.

"Is this how you see me?"

At first, she didn't know how to answer and then she said, "It's one of the masks you wear."

He paused for a moment and flipped to another picture of himself. He sat on her porch in Bellingham, flannel shirt open, jean clad legs stretched out in front of him. His face seemed younger, happier. He looked like a completely different person.

"The pictures don't mean anything. They're just drawings," Emma said and managed to snatch the pad out of his hands. "We all wear masks. We have to be different people in different parts of our lives."

"But how do you see me?"

"What?"

"You drew two images of me, but which one do you see me as?"

"You're both men, but your business side dominates everything else. That's not a bad thing. That's what you are."

He considered and nodded. "Business has dominated everything for over twelve years, but I'm trying to switch my focus. Do you know why I was in Bellingham when I met you?"

"You said you were on vacation," she ventured.

"I hit a breaking point when I got into a fight with a client and nearly punched him in the face. I was restless and angry and I couldn't concentrate. My doctor said my blood pressure was through the roof and if I didn't bring it down, I would work myself into an early grave. Derek kicked me out of the office until I got a hold of myself. I didn't know where to go, so I went to see Tommy and met you."

"You never told me that."

"You changed my focus for the first time in twelve years. For the first time, I was able to kick back and just… be. I was able to go back to work because I knew you would be there when I got back. Whenever the pressure chokes me, I visit you. You ground me."

She tried not to read too much into his words. "How's your blood pressure now?"

He shrugged. "It fluctuates. I know I need to change."

"I didn't know," she said quietly.

His dark eyes were piercing as they searched hers. "I had a talk with Anna and Tommy."

Dread fizzed through her. "About what?"

"Why didn't you tell me about your parents?"

Emma's body turned to stone. "What about them?"

"Why didn't you tell me how they died, *when* they died?"

"That's none of your business!"

Peter's eyes narrowed to slits. "Not my business? I suppose the fact that you were engaged to Ben once upon a time isn't my business either?"

"Damn right! I don't ask you about all the women in your past. We didn't have that kind of relationship!"

"What the hell kind of relationship did we have?" he demanded.

"The sexual kind! We didn't cuddle and talk about the future or past history."

"You never let me in! Not once did you tell me what was going on right in front of me. It wasn't just that I was absent. You don't think I'd understand what you went through with Ben and the accident?"

Emma turned and walked out of the cabin. She couldn't breathe. How could Anna and Tommy do this to her? She started towards the cliff, but didn't get far before Peter whirled her around. The cold wind whipped around them and Peter raised his voice to be heard over the sound of the waves below.

"Why didn't you tell me that the anniversary of the accident is the same week as our anniversary?" he demanded.

"What does it matter?"

"If I'd known—"

"*Then* you would have showed up because you felt sorry for me? No thanks!"

He shook her. "I could be there for you, you idiot!"

"I want you to be there because you want *me*, not because I'm going through a hard time! I can handle this on my own! Parents die, people betray you—" Her voice broke and her eyes burned with tears. "I didn't come here for this. I want to forget everything, I don't want to keep reliving it."

"It's a part of your history and you're making decisions based on what you lost," he said brutally.

"You think you know what happened just because someone told you bare facts? You have no idea how I feel, what I want!"

"What *do* you want?"

"I don't know anymore! I lost everything. I'm just trying to pick up the pieces."

"I can—"

She shook her head violently. "No."

"You don't have a choice," he snapped.

He picked her up and carried her back to the cabin. She was chilled to the bone and she trembled in his grasp. He sat on the couch and wrapped them both in blankets. She tried to get away from him, but he squeezed the life out of her. She had no choice but to settle against him.

"My mom dropped me off at my aunt's house when I was six," he said.

Emma stared straight ahead and did her best impression of a rock.

"She never came back for me." Peter buried his face in her hair and breathed deep. "My aunt hated me. She didn't have any kids of her own, but she put food on the table and gave me clothes to wear. She never let me forget that I was a burden and that I should be grateful that she gave me a place to stay."

Emma opened her mouth to speak, but snapped it shut and listened.

"I was good at sports. I managed to get a scholarship to a private high school. My aunt grumbled even though she didn't have to pay anything. I met Derek and his parents began to take me with them on vacations. They paid my way to college. They're the reason I'm where I am today."

Peter squeezed Emma and rested his chin on her shoulder.

"I know what it's like to be left behind, to be betrayed by someone you love," he murmured. "I don't know where my mom is or what happened to her. At this point in my life, I don't care."

"I'm sorry."

"It was hard as a kid. You wonder what's wrong with you, why God did this to me. I grew up faster than most kids, but I turned out okay. I vowed I'd never let anyone mean so much to me, so if they left, I wouldn't care."

She nodded, but didn't comment. He rubbed his face in her hair and goose bumps broke out over her skin. His hand splayed over her stomach and she dug her nails into his skin in warning, but the hand didn't move up or down.

"You're the first person to break through to me since Derek," he confessed.

She blinked and a tear slid down her cheek. "Peter, you don't have to—"

"Yes, I do. I was so busy trying to keep my walls up that I didn't see you had your own demons. I'm sorry."

"I can't talk about it."

"I don't know how got through losing your parents... and what happened with Ben. How can you go through what you went through and leave yourself open?"

The unspoken 'Why did you let yourself love me?' made her mouth quirk in a sad smile. "You barged into my life and distracted me during the worst time of year for me. How could I hold back from you?"

Peter nipped her neck. "I knew you were trouble the minute I saw you."

"Ditto."

His hold tightened on her. "You're afraid to give me

another chance because I held back before. I won't anymore. I can't change the past, but I'm here now."

"I don't think—"

"You don't have to make any decisions right now. I think we both need to figure out what we want."

~

*E*mma woke in her bedroom as the sun set, coloring the room in orange light. She had a vague recollection of Peter carrying her here when she dozed off in his arms. The fact that Peter knew about her past made everything so much more complicated. Did he come on this trip because he felt guilty? She didn't want or need Peter here, injecting her heart with hope. Why not just let her go?

She reached for her cell and dialed Anna's number. She answered on the second ring.

"Emma how's everything?"

"Why did you tell Peter about the accident?" Emma couldn't hold back the anger in her voice.

There was a startled pause and then a sigh, "He deserves to know, Emma. He came to my house to get drunk after Georgina's wedding. He wants to make it work and he keeps coming back to you even when you push him away."

"Anna, you had no right."

"I'm sorry. I did what I thought was best."

"I'll talk to you later," Emma said and hung up.

She showered and changed into sweats. She looked in the mirror. The strain she felt was written all over her face. She gave Anna her reasons for breaking up with Peter. Hadn't Anna agreed with her? So, what if Peter decided to get drunk after she turned him away? She scowled at her reflection. Had they arrived only yesterday? It felt like a week.

"Emma?" Peter's voice came through the door.

"Yes?"

"I have dinner ready."

She finished her hair and walked into the kitchen and found the table set with steaming meatloaf, vegetables and mashed potatoes. Peter poured a glass of wine for each of them. When she hesitated, he pulled out her chair.

"Sit."

She sat and noticed her sketchpad on the table. He made their plates and sat across from her. She took a gulp of wine and dug into the meal. The food settled her stomach and when she finished, she sipped her wine.

"Anna and Tommy love you," he began, reading the tension in her body.

"That doesn't mean they know what's best for me," she said coolly.

"They told me about the accident so I'd understand."

"It wasn't for them to tell."

"Would you have told me?"

"No."

A muscle flexed in his jaw. "Hearing about the accident shows me I did everything wrong where you're concerned."

"It just shows me we're not meant for each other. You have your life in Seattle and I have mine in Bellingham. You're never going to change, Peter."

Peter said nothing and she twisted the stem of her wine glass between her fingers.

"I didn't know about your background," she said to change the subject. "It's amazing what you've done for yourself."

"It's common knowledge that my aunt raised me, but only Derek knows what it was like for me to live with her. Derek's parents saved my life."

"His parents must be proud of you."

"They are. I don't like needing people."

She sighed. "I don't see the point in this. Once we get back to the real world, you're going to spend just as much time in Seattle."

"I can switch my schedule around."

Emma rolled her eyes and took another sip of wine.

"There's one thing I want to know," Peter said.

"What?"

"Is Ben the reason you broke up with me?"

"What do you mean?"

"You think if he loved and left you, there's no chance in hell I'll stay. Am I right?"

"I don't know why you'd keep coming back to someone you *didn't* love." She speared a hand through her hair. "None of this matters now."

"I can understand how forgetting about you on our anniversary shook you up. It won't happen again."

She shook her head. "Before the accident, I had work and family. Now, I have Anna, but the time I used to spend with family I spend working because there's nothing to go home to. When we were together, my work hours didn't change because you were never around! I want to be in a relationship where the guy is present."

"I can change."

"You're not the relationship type. I knew that when I met you. You wouldn't be happy playing full time boyfriend," Emma muttered.

"I enjoy our time together."

"Until you get restless and run back to the city."

He didn't deny that.

Emma eyed him doubtfully over the rim of her glass. "While we're here, no sex."

He drank his wine and didn't answer.

*T*he week passed by surprisingly fast. Emma tried to ignore Peter and secretly hoped he'd get frustrated and leave. He didn't. He spent a lot of time on his laptop in the kitchen and went on daily hikes up and down the cliffs. She stayed inside and cleaned the cabin, painted her nails and drew elaborate wedding cakes for a catalog she wanted to put together. She made sure she checked her email every now and then, but Anna had things under control. Emma ignored the apologies that peppered the emails from her friend. She blamed Anna and Tommy for her current dilemma. Being stuck in a cabin with Peter Logan wasn't her idea of a restful vacation.

Peter didn't try to seduce her and showed no signs of frustration with his forced abstinence. This offended Emma. Didn't he want her anymore? Bastard. The pseudo platonic relationship between them took a toll on her. All she could think about was jumping him and the resulting sketches were thrown in the fireplace before he spotted them. She tossed and turned at night and considered cutting her vacation short just to get out of this predicament, but pride forced her to stay. She could handle being around Peter and not having sex with him, right?

CHAPTER 11

*I*n the beginning of the second week, the tension in the cabin became thicker with every passing hour. Emma spent more and more time in her room with the door closed because it was the best way to avoid Peter and the way he watched her. They were both tense and she was beginning to feel the effects of cabin fever, which put her in a nasty mood.

When Peter knocked on the door and told her he was going to the store, she almost wept in relief. As soon as she heard the SUV leave, she burst out of her room with her sketchpad under her arm. She walked outside and took deep breaths of the frigid air. She needed peace and quiet and couldn't do it with Peter hovering around her. She headed down the steep path to the pebble beach below. She perched on a rock, raised her face to the ocean mist that caressed her face and got to work.

Time ran away from her. She sketched until her fingers cramped. She looked down at the images of Peter and her parents. She wondered what her parents would think of him. Her mom wouldn't approve since he was a workaholic. For the first time, Emma understood why her mom griped about her work life. What good was money when you didn't have the time to do anything with it? She had both bakeries up and running, a comfortable income and no family or personal life. She wanted someone to share her life with.

Emma set her sketch pad aside, stretched and turned her back to the ocean to look up the cliff and wondered if Peter was back. A wave slammed into her with such force that she fell on her hands and knees on the rocks. Emma went down hard and was too stunned to fight when the wave retreated, pulling her into the ocean. She thrashed and swallowed mouthfuls of water before she realized which way was up. When she broke through the surface, she was sucked into the undertow. She kicked with all her might and made it onto shore, sputtering and coughing up seawater.

Shaking convulsively, she looked around and realized the tide crept in while she drew. Emma scrambled towards the cliff and stumbled her way up the steep path, gagging and moaning from the cold. She was nearly at the top when she heard Peter calling her name. She tried to call out to him, but her throat was dry and she thought she was in danger of freezing to death. His voice got closer and it was the most welcome sound she ever heard.

"What the hell happened?" he shouted.

Peter slid to a stop in front of her and hauled her into his arms. She moaned and buried her numb face on his chest as he hustled her back to the cabin.

"You're going to get sick," he thundered.

He shoved his way into her bathroom and began to strip off her sodden clothes. She opened her mouth to protest, but her teeth chattered too hard for her to speak. Peter turned on the shower and she blinked in surprise when he stripped and stepped in with her. She had no choice but to lean against him as the hot water beat down on her back.

"Look at your hands," he snapped.

She had several cuts, which trickled blood down her arms. She flinched when he put her palms under the unforgiving spray. She bit his bare chest. He ignored her and muttered under his breath as he soaped her hair and body. She let him tend to her because she was shell-shocked and the feel of his hands felt like heaven. Too soon, Peter hauled her out of the tub and roughly dried her. He wrapped her in a robe and fetched his own before he dragged her in front of the fireplace. She shivered while he got it going. When it blazed to life, he placed her so close that her face felt singed, but she was too grateful to argue. Peter rummaged around in the kitchen and reappeared with water, tea and soup. He watched her through narrow eyes as she drank the whole glass of water to get the salty taste out of her mouth. The soup made her feel waterlogged, but she ate it all.

Peter brought out a first aid kit and cupped her hands in his. "What happened?"

"Turned my back on the water."

"Bad mistake."

She yanked her hand back. "I know that."

"You could have drowned!"

"I know that too."

"You shouldn't go to the beach by yourself."

She glared. "I grew up here. I'm not an idiot. I just... forgot. I'm fine now."

"You could've been swept out to sea and—"

"But I didn't."

He got to his feet and paced. She watched him warily. She could feel his temper boiling beneath the surface and his hands clenched and unclenched at his sides.

"You are the most stubborn person I have ever met," he hissed as he passed by.

"You're just as stubborn. You don't know the meaning of the word no," she retorted.

Peter dropped to his knees in front of her, grasped her by the shoulders and shook her. "I know when something's a lost cause. I also know when something is good. If you'd stop being such a hard ass, I could show you that. Give me a second chance!"

She shoved him back. "Why don't you find someone else?"

"Because I want *you*! We click and damn it, you love me!" When Emma looked away, he grasped her chin and forced her to meet his burning eyes. "Don't you?"

"Leave me alone."

"I can't. Even when we're done here, I'm going to be on your doorstep, pounding on your door until you let me in."

He was breathing hard and his hands shook. She stared at him and her heart skipped a beat.

"What do you want?" she whispered.

He cupped the back of her head and held her still as his lips covered hers. She felt the urgency, frustration and temper in him. Her lips softened as his moved over hers. She opened her mouth and clutched the edges of his robe. Peter pulled away and dropped his head on her shoulder. He stayed that way for several minutes.

"I want you."

His hands smoothed over her sides and gripped her hips.

"We both have our secrets," he murmured against her neck. "Now they're gone and we can start over."

"I don't see how—"

Peter pressed his finger to her lips and raised his head. His eyes were narrow and bright. "You trust me with your body, but nothing else." He ran his finger over her bottom lip. "You don't play games and you love me. I was so pissed when you broke up with me. I care, Emma."

He shushed her when she tried to speak. His finger left a trail of fire in its wake as he ran it down her throat and between her breasts.

"You're not willing to take the chance because of Ben, but I won't walk away. You handled the accident and the death of your parents alone. I want to be here for you. Let me."

Her heart pounded into overdrive. She gripped his shoulders as emotion kicked through her with the force of a shot of tequila.

"I don't have much left," she whispered. "If this doesn't work I—"

Peter cupped her face. "I won't fail this time."

Tears stung her eyes as he laid her in front of the fire. His hands were reverent and they trembled as they moved over her skin. He kissed his way down her body until he reached the heart of her. She twisted the soft rug beneath her and screamed. He slid into her as she climaxed. The firelight played over his skin as he moved over her. He thrust in and out of her and she felt the claim he was staking. She gave herself to him and prayed she wasn't heading towards more heartbreak.

~

*E*mma stared into the flames. Peter trapped her legs with a heavy thigh and his arm draped over her waist. She knew he was awake, but neither of them spoke. She must have dozed off after the second climax because when she came to, she was in the bedroom. Sex with Peter short-circuited her brain. She wasn't sure if that was a good or bad thing.

Peter let her nap, fed her and seduced her again. Night fell and the only light came from the fire. Peter touched and kissed her as if he were starved for her. She felt consumed by him. Her lips were swollen and her body felt pleasantly used, but her mind ricocheted with conflicting thoughts.

"It's going to be okay, Emma," Peter murmured.

She took a deep breath. "I was driving that night."

Peter's hand tightened on her hip. He didn't interrupt or force her to face him. She never talked about the accident, but she felt compelled to tell him.

"My parents were in the back seat. This guy had car trouble and had nowhere to pull off the road. I came around the corner and slammed on the brakes. The car behind rear ended us and we plowed into the car in front." Her eyes blurred with tears, but she forced herself to finish. "My dad died instantly. My mom got thrown from the car. She had bits of the car door stuck in her." She took a shaky breath. "I held her against me and told Ben to help me stop the bleeding." She closed her eyes as pain shredded her insides. "He said he couldn't deal with it and walked away from me. I rocked my mom in my arms until she died. I checked the other cars. No one else survived."

Peter held her tight when she trembled. "It's not your fault, Emma."

"I don't know why we survived and no one else did," she whispered.

"It's meant to be."

Her nails dug into the rug. "I never forgave Ben. I needed him and he just walked away from me. I thought he loved me and…"

He ran his hands over her suddenly chilled skin. "You survived, Emma."

A tear trickled down her cheek. "If it hadn't been for Anna, I don't know how I would've made it through. I tried to move on and when the anniversary came around, you showed up and you wouldn't leave me alone. Thank you for that."

"I wish I'd known."

She turned in his arms and placed her hands over his heart. "If this doesn't work out—"

"It will."

"If you want out—"

"Emma, shut up."

He pushed her onto her back and kissed her tears away. He worshipped her body and when she screamed his name, he slid into her and met her eyes.

"Trust me this time," he whispered.

She kissed him and he took over. Nightmares didn't intrude when she fell asleep in his arms.

⤳

For the next two weeks, they were inseparable. The tension in the cabin disappeared overnight. For the first time, Emma felt truly at ease with Peter. They fell into a routine. They woke up and took care of business in the morning before they walked along the cliff or down to the beach. Peter enjoyed feeding her and took advantage of the time to break the invisible barriers between them and learn how she liked her coffee and what her favorite flower was. Emma was cautiously beginning to hope that this could work.

"Would you consider moving to the city?" Peter asked one night when they lay in bed.

Emma stiffened in surprise. "What?"

"You want to see more of me, right?"

"I guess," she said and yelped when he bit her. "Okay, yes."

"I want you to move in with me."

"I don't think I want to move to the city," she said warily.

"Okay, then I'll move in with you." It was what he'd been hoping for anyway.

"What?"

"We've been together for over a year."

"Yes, but—"

"This is the next step in our relationship. I have the penthouse, but I like your house. I'm going to be there every weekend."

Remembering his broken promises from the past she said, "Shouldn't we ease back into being a couple?"

"No, we're over a year into our relationship. It's time for some kind of commitment, right?"

"I don't need—"

"Fine, *I* need a commitment. I told you I was going to change my work schedule and work on my new goals."

"And what are your new goals?"

"To have a life with you outside of the office. We should come here more often. I've never done this kind of stuff before. Derek and Tommy were the first people that believed in me, that expected me to go further than I thought possible. I built up an empire so I'd have something no one could take away from me. It's built and now I can figure out what else I want." He looked down at her body. "I definitely want you, so I'll focus on you and see where we go from there."

"Peter, you're so romantic."

"I'll work on it." He slapped her butt when she tried to muffle her giggles. "This time, you'll tell me what you need, right?"

Another butt slap before she said, "Yes, sir."

"I like the sound of that," he growled and pounced on her.

CHAPTER 12

"I can't believe it's over," Emma said as she leaned back against Peter.

He wrapped his arms around her. She saw Seattle rise out of the fog as the ferry approached. It felt as if they'd been gone for a year rather than a month. Being around all these people after being isolated for so long was overwhelming.

"We'll come back soon," Peter said.

She felt great. She felt rested and… content? She was ready to go back to work and she believed Peter changed. He spent a month with her at the cabin, which shocked the hell out of her. More stunning was the fact that he'd actually enjoyed himself, but they were both ready to go back to work. A tiny voice inside of her murmured, *now we'll really see if anything's changed.*

"Are you sure you can come this weekend? We both have a lot to catch up on," she hedged.

"I'll be there Friday," he said firmly.

She was tempted to pursue the issue, but when he shot her a chiding look, she subsided. The ferry docked and Peter kept her hand twined in his when they disembarked. He reluctantly walked her to the hotel parking lot where she left her car. She leaned back against the driver's door and he caged her in.

"Do you have to go back right now?"

"Yes."

He groaned. "You're a hard ass."

She grinned, feeling more lighthearted than she had in years. She liked the new bantering between them. Before, they'd always been too busy trying to hold one another at a distance to laugh. The time they spent together in Victoria created this new intimacy between them that infected her with hope for their future together.

Peter kissed and tucked her into the car. She honked and wove her way out of Seattle, mind sifting through her trip with Peter. He promised things would be different and she wanted to believe him. A niggle of doubt rose. Would their bond last in the real world with distance, distractions and business? Were they on the same page now or was this a temporary fix? Today was Saturday. They had six days away from each other before he was supposed to come back to Bellingham. That was six days for him to go back to his real life and put her in second place again.

She pushed all of that to the side. There was nothing she could do about it. Only time would tell and she promised him she would try. By the time she reached Bellingham, she was ready to see her house and sleep in her own bed. Although she felt as if she'd gone through a life changing experience, everything looked the same, which was comforting. She carried her bags into the house, started a load of laundry and ordered a pizza.

Her cell rang and she hesitated. "Hey, Anna."

"Are you home?" Anna's voice was unnaturally high.

"Yes. What's—?"

"I'll be there in five minutes."

The line went dead. She stared at the phone for a second, but decided that the sooner they talked, the better. She hadn't talked to Anna since she confronted her friend about telling Peter her secret. She couldn't be too mad at Anna since everything worked out with Peter, but what it if hadn't? Emma accepted the steaming pizza from the delivery guy and headed into the kitchen. She heard Anna's key in the lock a moment before the front door banged open. Emma walked into the living room with a frown on her face. Anna's purse drooped from one shoulder and she held a grocery bag filled to the brim with rectangle boxes. She was milk pale and the shirt she wore gaped because she hadn't buttoned it correctly.

"What's wrong?" Emma demanded.

Anna looked as if she were fighting tears. "Do you hate me?"

"No. You were right, I should have told him. Are you okay?"

Anna burst into tears and threw herself into Emma's arms.

"I just wanted to help," Anna sobbed.

Emma patted her back. "You did. I have to thank you—"

"No!" Anna jerked away and threw herself on the couch. "Don't thank me. I shouldn't be in anyone's business, as Tommy likes to tell me."

Emma perched near Anna who clutched the grocery bag to her chest like a Bible. "Anna, what's going on? You're scaring me."

Anna turned tear-drenched eyes on her. "Do you forgive me?"

"Of course. I just needed time. What's going on? You look horrible."

"The day you left, Tommy and I got into a huge fight."

"You and Tommy?" Emma couldn't believe it. They were the perfect couple. "What did you guys fight about?"

"His socks," Anna wailed.

"Socks?"

"He doesn't fold them!" Anna snapped and began to pace, still clutching the grocery bag. "He said if he doesn't fold his socks that's his choice and I said, 'Oh no it's not! If you don't fold your socks, you can move into a different bedroom.'"

Emma blinked and cleared her throat. "I don't understand."

Anna didn't even hear Emma. Her eyes were wild as she stomped around the living room. This was so out of character for Anna that Emma stared in amazement.

"I don't know what came over me. I started ripping his socks out of the drawer and throwing them in the guest bedroom. He asked if I was having my period and I went berserk. I grabbed all his clothes and threw them in the guest room too. He left the house and didn't come back for two days!"

"Oh my God," Emma said.

"I came home from work and he's sitting at the table drinking a beer as if he never left. I tried to apologize, but he didn't want to hear it. He said I'm a controlling workaholic. Whenever I try to talk to him, he tells me to go back to the bakery. Tommy's been living in the guest bedroom for over a month. He goes to work and stays out all night."

Anna shook uncontrollably. Emma wrapped an arm around her friend and felt like crap for not talking to her.

"This was just a stupid fight," Emma soothed. "You guys can work it out."

"No, we can't," Anna said in a muffled voice. "He said he wants a divorce."

"*Over socks?* He can't do that. You guys are made for each other."

Anna let out a weary laugh. "Apparently not. I've been having these crazy mood swings and—"

"Oh my God, you should have told me to come back!"

Anna held up a hand. "No, you needed your time and I can handle this, but today I thought of something."

Anna took a deep breath and jiggled the grocery bag. A pregnancy test fell to the ground. Emma stared at it, uncomprehending, before she let out a scream.

"You're pregnant?" Emma shouted, overjoyed and scared to death.

"I don't know!" Anna screamed back and dropped the bag. Pregnancy tests from every brand known to man scattered across the floor.

"Have you taken one yet?" Emma demanded.

"No! I couldn't do it alone. I wanted to wait until you came back."

"I'm here. You can do this."

It took Emma thirty minutes to get Anna to take the test. She wrung her hands outside the bathroom door, trying to come to grips with everything. Anna and Tommy, the ideal couple, were on the verge of divorce and Anna could be pregnant. She could be an aunt. Emma had to sit on the bed because she was completely overwhelmed. Anna came out of the bathroom and they sat together, hands clasped as they stared at the pregnancy test on the counter.

"Everything's going to be okay," Emma whispered.

"Is it?" Anna whispered.

"It is! You know why? Because I'm here and Tommy loves you."

"You don't see the way he looks at me," Anna moaned.

"You didn't see the way Peter looked at me when I pushed him away. It gave me nightmares."

Hope lit Anna's eyes. "Are you two…?"

Emma couldn't stop the smile, despite Anna's despair. "We are."

Anna squeezed her hands. "I knew it. Peter's so in love with you. He wasn't going to let you go."

"He doesn't love me," Emma corrected. "He cares for me."

"Emma," Anna gave her a reproachful look. "Would a guy who *cares* for you go this far to prove himself?"

"Peter's an overachiever."

"He loves you," Anna said firmly. "I can see it. That's why I told him about the accident. He deserved to know."

"It's time," Emma broke in. "Are you ready?"

"No."

"Do you want to be pregnant?" Emma asked gently.

Anna started to cry again. "No! Tommy said he doesn't want to be tied to me. Never once in our marriage has he mentioned kids! Never!"

So, it wasn't just her and Peter that had their guards up. "And you've always wanted kids."

"Eventually," Anna admitted. "But, I wasn't going to ask him if I could go off birth control. If he wanted a kid with me, he would have brought it up, right? *Right?*"

Emma held her hands up. "Maybe you aren't pregnant. We have to look."

"Okay, you do it. I don't think I can walk."

Emma's heart pounded as if this were her own pregnancy test. She stopped in the doorway of the bathroom for a long minute before she went over to the counter and read the tiny letters. She slowly turned to face Anna.

"It's positive."

Anna surged up from the bed and snatched the test. "This has to be a mistake!" Her eyes were wide with fear. "This can't happen. I'm not ready. I'm getting divorced."

"You're not divorced yet. Your hormones are going crazy because you're pregnant. Tommy can't hold that against you."

Anna grasped Emma by the shoulders and shook her. "I don't want Tommy to stay with me because of the baby! And I can't be a mother, I'd turn into mine and I can't stand her. I'm on the pill. You can't get pregnant while you're on the pill, right?"

"I—" Emma twisted her hands together. "I'm not sure."

"I'm going to be the worst mother ever! I'm too controlling just like Tommy said."

Anna crumpled dramatically to the floor. Worried for the baby, Emma put her arms around her friend and persuaded her to lay in her bed.

"Anna, pull yourself together. Maybe the test is wrong. Let's take another one."

"Will you take one for me?" Anna pleaded. "If yours is negative, I'll know I'm really pregnant."

"I don't know," Emma said uneasily.

"Do it!" Anna snapped.

"Okay, okay," Emma brushed Anna's hair back from her face. "Okay, I'll take one."

She calmed the hysterical expectant mother and peed on the stick. While they waited for the results, she went downstairs and grabbed sodas and pizza and brought it up to Anna who ate ravenously.

"I think it's ready. Give it to me easy," Anna said, closing her eyes as Emma walked into the bathroom.

Emma looked down at her own test and stilled.

"Emma?"

She turned slowly to face her friend and was dimly aware of a faint buzzing in her ears. "It's positive. There must be something wrong with this brand."

Anna sat bolt upright, face shifting from misery to amazement. "Are you—?"

"No! I can't be. I'm on the pill," Emma's voice was shrill with fear.

"Don't panic." Anna rushed to Emma who shook life a lead and resumed her role as a mother figure. "We'll try a different brand. Maybe neither of us is pregnant."

They gulped down their sodas and tried three different brands. They were all positive. Emma was stunned.

"It's going to be okay," Anna consoled her.

"I'm not even married. I just got back together with Peter. Is he gonna think I did this on purpose?" Emma asked numbly.

"Of course not. Peter loves you."

"And Tommy loves you," Emma shot back and Anna flinched.

"What are we going to do?"

"We're gonna have babies."

They stared at one another and suddenly the fear of how their men would respond was banished by wonder and joy. They clung to each other and laughed and cried.

"What if I have a boy and you have a girl and they fall in love?" Anna said.

"I don't think either of us would survive. I hope we both have girls that are best friends."

Anna started to cry. "Aww."

Emma began to cry too. "I know!"

Overexcited and overstressed, Anna fell asleep not long after. Emma lay beside her for an hour before she walked downstairs and sat at the kitchen table, staring straight ahead. She patted her flat stomach while her mind raced. How? When? She drove back to Bellingham, believing that nothing changed yet within the hour her life had turned upside down. Giving Peter a second chance had been a huge step for her and now this. She tried to imagine Peter's reaction to the news. Her stomach pitched. When her cell rang, she was relieved to see Tommy's name instead of Peter's.

"Yes?" Emma answered coolly.

"Is Anna with you? She's not at home," Tommy said, sounding distracted.

"Why are you home? It's only five."

"What's that supposed to mean?"

"I thought you've been staying out all night. You haven't been worried about where your wife is any other night."

Emma thought of Anna's fears about being a bad mother. Instead of being here to comfort her, Tommy enhanced Anna's belief that she was a horrible person. So, what if Anna wanted things done a certain way? She went out of her way to make sure that Tommy was comfortable and happy. He never complained when Anna made sure there was a cold beer on the table with his dinner.

"Just tell me if she's with you," Tommy said through gritted teeth.

"She is. Have you filed for divorce yet?"

A long pause. "She told you?"

"Yes. She's going to move in with me, so you can have the house."

"What? Over my dead body!" Tommy shouted. "We're still married—"

"You said she's a controlling workaholic and don't want to be tied to her. She's accepted it, so you can fax the divorce papers when you have a chance."

Emma knew she was taking a huge chance on her friend's marriage, but she had faith in Tommy. She loved him like a brother and if he was going to be a good father, he damn well better give her the right answers. Now.

"She's gonna give up just like that?" His outrage was clear.

"Why should she stay in a marriage where her husband hates her?" Emma challenged.

"I don't hate her!"

"Send the papers when you have a chance," Emma said and hung up on him.

CHAPTER 13

*P*eter was up to his elbows in emails and files. People kept coming into the office to ask him about clients, accounts they weren't sure about and emails that hadn't been answered. No one hid their relief that he was back. In his absence, Derek turned into a tyrant. Peter enjoyed his time in Victoria because of Emma, but couldn't deny that the frantic pace at work made his blood race.

His cell, which he made sure was nearby with the volume turned up, began to ring. He set the files down immediately and frowned when he saw Tommy's name.

"Hey, Tommy. What's up?"

"What's up?"

Tommy's voice was so loud that Peter jerked the phone away from his ear.

"What's up is Anna wants a divorce."

Peter nearly dropped the phone. "What?"

"I was trying to teach her a lesson, you know, get her attention off the bakery. We had a stupid fight and it snowballed out of control. I threatened to divorce her and now that Emma's back, Anna moved in with her."

"You threatened Anna with divorce?" Peter couldn't believe it. "And Anna moved in with Emma?"

"I don't know how the hell this happened. Emma told me to fax the divorce papers. Anna's not even going to fight for our marriage?" Tommy yelled.

"You're the one that told me they're alike. They don't take crap from us. Did you try to fix things with Anna?"

Tommy didn't answer.

"You better go over there and get down on your knees," Peter advised, "before Emma convinces Anna to sign the papers and have them sent to you."

"Shit," Tommy said and the line went dead.

Peter checked his phone, but he didn't have any calls from Emma. He dialed her number and smiled when she picked up.

"Peter?" she sounded uncertain.

"Hey, babe. Tommy just called me."

A long pause. "He did?"

He laughed. "Expect him in the next hour. Record him. This may be the only time he'll beg in his life."

"He better get over here," Emma said, her voice growing stronger. "They're married and she needs him. They belong together."

"Is Anna okay?"

Another pause. "She will be."

"Are you okay?"

"Sure. Why?"

"Dealing with a married couple's problems isn't the best homecoming."

A strained laugh. "Yeah, I wasn't expecting this... any of it."

"Tommy loves Anna. He's not going to leave without her."

"That's good. He needs to tell her he's going to support her no matter what."

Peter frowned. Emma sounded tense, strained and worried. The woman he kissed and waved off a couple hours ago was gone. Had dealing with Anna and Tommy changed her mood or was something else wrong?

"He'll support her no matter what," Peter confirmed.

"But, what if something happens that she can't control? Will he still support her if it's not part of the plan? What if he accuses her of lying?"

"Did she cheat on him?" Peter asked sharply.

"What? No!" Emma snapped. "Did *he* cheat on her?"

"No! There's no cheating involved. They'll settle their differences."

"I hear Anna upstairs. I better go talk to her about what I did."

"You lied about her agreeing to the divorce?" He wasn't surprised.

"Tommy asked for one and Anna was going to give it to him. I just called his bluff."

She didn't sound the least bit sorry. Emma was definitely going to keep him on his toes.

"Remind me never to threaten you with a divorce," he said and hated the long pause on the other end.

"I don't think you and I will ever have that problem."

"You don't think so?" he challenged. She never thought they'd get to the altar? Where did she think their relationship was going?

"I have to go," Emma said quickly.

"No, Emma. This isn't like before when I never called, when we didn't talk. If you need something, you tell me. You understand?" He couldn't keep the anger out of his voice. He was damned if he was going to go back to being unsure of her again.

"Things happen—"

"And couples stay together. Tommy and Anna will make it through and so will you and I. Got it?"

She took a deep breath. "Okay."

"You and I are together. That's all that matters."

"Peter, how rich are you?"

If it had been any other woman, he would have been alarmed, but this was Emma and she sounded sad, as if the fact that he was wealthy was a bad thing.

"I don't have to work for the rest of my life."

"Has anyone ever tried to blackmail you for money?" she asked hesitantly.

"The aunt I told you about."

"What?" Emma was outraged. "After abandoning you, she wanted money? You better not have paid her!"

Peter grinned. Emma was careful not to crowd him in the past, but he would make sure that changed. He liked how protective she was of him, even when he could fend for himself. Emma and Anna were so similar. If both of them were determined to do something, God help anyone who stood in their way.

"I didn't pay her a cent. I don't have respect for people that would do that to any child."

"Oh," Emma said thoughtfully. "I have to go. Tommy will be here soon."

"Okay, Emma. I'll see you on Friday."

"Yes. I'll see you then. Bye."

≈

*L*ong after Tommy took Anna home, Emma lay in bed. The five positive pregnancy tests were lined up on her nightstand. She drifted in and out of sleep and each time she woke, she got up to look at each test to make sure it was still true.

Before the sun rose, Emma was in the office at the bakery. The building was empty and silent. It was just her and the work. She wasn't surprised that she hadn't heard from Anna. Last night while Tommy pounded on the front door, Emma explained to Anna what incited him to come looking for her. Far from being angry, Anna congratulated her friend on being a great strategist. Emma stayed in the kitchen and listened to them fight. By the end of the hour, Emma felt sorry for Tommy. Anna hadn't revealed her ace card and Emma wondered when she would tell Tommy the news. Anna was confident Peter would take the baby in stride, but, how could he? He wanted a girlfriend, not a family.

Emma took a break from the computer and made a pot of coffee. Asking Peter about being blackmailed hadn't fazed him. How could his aunt ask for money? After his childhood, how would he feel about having a child? She'd been so close to asking him to drive to Bellingham last night, but she held back. She needed time to think about this. Having a child was… amazing, scary and life changing. Every child needed a father. She thought of her own and sniffed back tears. She wished her mom were here.

She ambled back into her office and got back to work. She received several texts from Peter, which was unprecedented. He complained about his business partner, Derek, who blamed Peter for not being able to get laid for over a month because he'd been working too much. At three, Emma left the bakery and was surprised to see a moving truck in her driveway. Two men sat in the cab, talking.

"You have the right address?" Emma asked, coming up to the driver's window.

"Are you Emma?"

"Yeah."

"Peter Logan hired us to bring his stuff to this address."

Emma gaped. He was serious about moving in? But, what if he changed his mind after he heard about the baby?

The men in overalls jumped out and lifted the back of the truck. It was filled with boxes. While the men started stacking boxes, she called Peter.

"Hey, babe."

"Peter, the movers are here," she hissed.

"Good. They're on time. Just show them our bedroom."

"Peter, I—" she floundered. "Are you sure about this?"

"Yes."

No hesitation or doubt.

"But—"

"But what?"

"I wasn't expecting this so soon."

"We talked about this at the cabin."

"I know, but—"

"You're just putting off the inevitable."

She swallowed as both movers started carrying boxes onto the porch. "Maybe I am. Why didn't you tell me you were sending your stuff here?"

"Because I knew you would react this way."

"You knew?" she screeched.

"I told you, things are different this time around."

"I can see you're taking that to heart."

"You should too."

She swallowed tears. If she wanted her baby to have a father, kicking him out when he was trying to establish himself in her life wasn't a good start.

"Okay, I'll call you later," she said.

She directed the movers into their room and when they offered to unpack the boxes, she declined. After they left, she sat on the bed and stared at Peter's boxes and then the pregnancy tests on the nightstand. How was this going to work?

*S*eeing her coworkers on Monday was a happy, but strained event. Workers and locals wanted to know where she'd gone, why and if she was seeing Peter Logan again. Anna came into work, glowing. Apparently, Tommy fulfilled Anna's every whim and he was over the moon about the baby.

"He said he always wanted kids, he was just waiting for me to say I wanted them too. He thought the bakery was getting in the way of us starting a family—that's why he was so mad at me," Anna said as she perched on Emma's desk.

"I'm happy for you."

"Did you tell Peter?"

"I'm seeing him on Friday. I couldn't tell him over the phone."

"I casually asked Tommy what Peter thought of kids. He said Peter donates to several children's charities and he's paid tuition for ten college students." Anna squeezed her hands. "Peter is a great guy."

"I know. He put up with me at my worst," Emma said.

"He loves you, that's why!" Anna insisted.

"He said things would be different this time around. I hope so. Have you made your doctor's appointment?"

"It's tomorrow. I made sure ours were right after the other."

Emma blew out a long breath and tried to ignore the way her heart fluttered with nerves. "I need to have it confirmed before I tell Peter."

"*You're* a little over two months," the doctor said.

Anna squeezed Emma's cold hands.

"We must have gotten pregnant the same week," Anna squealed.

"It was the day before I broke up with him," Emma said numbly.

So many emotions rushed through her. Excitement, fear, worry, hope. Anna bounced around the doctor's office, high as a kite. She just had her checkup and was indeed pregnant and healthy. She chattered happily through Emma's exam and linked arms with her as they headed out to the parking lot.

"So, how are you going to tell Peter?" Anna asked.

"How?"

"You know, are you going to give him a card with a poem, bake a cake with a rattle on it or put a bun in the oven? Oh, I once saw a girl on YouTube make this scavenger hunt—"

Emma turned to her friend. "I can't believe I'm pregnant, much less think how I'm supposed to explain this to Peter."

"This should be fun, though," Anna pouted.

"It should be." Emma leaned against the car to catch her breath.

"Oh my God. Are you okay?"

Anna patted her on the back as Emma gasped for air. A keening cry escaped from Emma and she turned to Anna for a hug. Anna didn't disappoint. She rocked her from side to side and whispered all the things she needed to hear in her ear.

"What's wrong?" Anna asked.

"I want my mom," Emma whispered. "I wish she was here. I wish my baby had grandparents."

Anna started to cry too. "Your kid won't have grandparents, but they'll have godparents."

Emma smiled as she pulled away. "That's true. Anna, I'm terrified. I don't know if I can do this."

"You can. I'm here and you're stronger than you think. We'll take it one step at a time," Anna said bracingly.

"What if Peter—"

"If Peter turns out to be a jackass, I'll be here. You know that, right?"

Emma nodded and felt better. She'd been alone for so long and in seven months she would have a child...

∼

*B*y Thursday, Emma was a bundle of nerves. She kept touching her stomach, unable to believe a baby was growing inside of her. She had no idea how she was going to tell Peter. She was in bed reading pregnancy stuff when he called.

"I'm not going to make it to Bellingham tomorrow," he said.

Her heart sank. He couldn't do this to her again.

"There's a party I have to go to. Will you be my date?"

Emma jerked to attention. "What?"

"Derek set up this party to punish me and I have to attend. All our clients will be there. Will you come to Seattle? You can move some of your stuff here to get back at me."

He sounded so hopeful that she laughed.

"You're insane. How dressy is the party?"

"Very."

"What time?"

"Starts at eight. What time can you leave Bellingham?"

"Probably around two. Why?"

"Come to my office and I'll take you to my penthouse."

"Okay."

"There's probably going to be a lot of questions, a lot of

staring. Derek will probably make rude comments. He's jealous."

"I can handle it."

"That's my girl. I'll see you tomorrow."

Emma called Anna who brought several outfits to the bakery the following day. She chose a shimmering white backless gown with a flowing front and matching shoes. Even though her stomach was flat, she felt self-conscious.

"You look so beautiful," Anna said through tears. "It's the baby. I blame him."

"Him?" Emma raised her brows.

"I've always wanted a boy," Anna said with a shrug. "How do you feel?"

"Glad I don't have morning sickness and terrified of telling Peter. I'm kind of nervous about the party. I have no idea what to expect."

"You'll be fine."

Emma wore a loose top with a blazer and jeans on her drive to Seattle. She kept going over how she would tell him. She couldn't think of any intro to ease him into the idea. Since they had the party tonight, she figured tomorrow would be the best time to tell him since they had the whole day together. This was the first time she was going into his world. She could see where he worked and lived. She had no idea what to expect.

She pulled into the garage of Peter's building. The uniformed guard guided her to a stall beside Peter's BMW. She grabbed her purse and stared when the guard said he would escort her across the street to Peter's workplace. The friendly guard, Barry, chattered all the way across the street and into an impressive building made of glass. He spoke to another guard who monitored the elevators.

"This here is Peter Logan's lady," Barry said.

They ushered her into the elevator so fast, the next thing

she knew she was heading up to the forty-eighth floor. Her palms began to sweat. She was going to see Peter, her boyfriend and father of her baby. She knew he was rich, but escorts and every employee in the building jumping to do his bidding? That was over the top, right? When the doors opened, a woman stepped forward, hand extended. She was very attractive and wore a pinstriped pantsuit.

"I'm Pat, Mr. Logan's secretary. It's nice to meet you. If you'll follow me."

Three women sat behind a reception desk with beautiful floral arrangements. They eyed her with fixed smiles. Should she have dressed up to come to his office? People rushed everywhere, carrying folders and coffee. Peter employed all these people? Emma resisted the urge to run back to the elevator. Maybe she should have Googled Peter before she dated him.

"How did you know when I was going to be here?" Emma asked, desperate for a diversion.

"I was notified as soon as you entered the parking garage. When Barry put you in the elevator, he called to let me know," Pat answered.

"Does Peter know?"

"Mr. Logan's in a meeting right now."

"Oh. Maybe I should come back later." Emma came to a stop, trying to get a handle on her anxiety which was skyrocketing.

Pat turned. "Mr. Logan told me to notify him as soon as I get you to his office."

"But maybe—"

"And who is this?" A deep voice drawled.

Emma turned and raised her brows. The man before her was gorgeous and for some reason irritated with her even though she'd never met him before. He was tall and immaculately dressed without a hair out of place. From the way the workers scurried to their cubicles, she figured he must be a big boss, which could mean only one thing.

"You must be Derek," Emma said.

"And you're the baker chick."

"Excuse me?" Emma frowned.

"First Tommy and now Peter. I think Bellingham's cursed. I refuse to visit," Derek said sourly.

"I think that's best," Emma said sweetly and Pat coughed delicately.

"I can take it from here, Pat," Derek said and the secretary nodded and backed away. "Shall we?"

"Sure."

Emma walked down the now empty and silent hall with Derek. Why the hell did she agree to come to Seattle? Everyone was staring at her. She began to feel claustrophobic.

"Do you love him?" Derek asked.

She tripped on the lush carpet. "I don't think that's your business."

"His personal life affects the business and I'm the other half of that business. With you, he's either floating on air or a rabid bear. I need to know which he's going to be so I can plan my vacation."

"You can't blame his moods on me," Emma objected.

"I can. I figured it out a couple of months ago. This week he's been happy and productive. I want to keep him that way."

"You sound like his boss," Emma said, disgruntled and embarrassed.

"We're each other's bosses. So, what's it gonna be, sweetheart?"

Emma put her hands on hips. "Did Peter put you up to this?"

"No. He's gonna kill me if you tell him." Derek didn't seem worried about that outcome.

"I love him—" she began.

Derek held up a hand like a traffic cop. "That's all I need to know. I guess I can delay my vacation."

She tapped her foot. "Are you trying to insult me or are you like this normally?"

"I'm like this. I irritate the hell out of Peter and Tommy, but I butter up the clients, so what are you gonna do?"

"Since we'll be running into each other, I guess you should call me something other than 'baker chick.' I'm Emma."

She held out a hand and he shook it.

"Derek. Does this mean you're moving to Seattle?"

"No. Peter moved some of his things in with me."

Derek looked pained. "What is *with* that town? It's taking the best businessmen out of the city."

"It's not the town, it's the women."

Derek gave her a once over. "Bellingham does seem to produce some fine women."

"Oh Derek, you're so romantic. You better take me to Peter's office quick before I set my sights on you." She couldn't believe this insulting, arrogant ass was easing her nerves.

His mouth twitched and his eyes warmed a fraction. "One, Peter would kill me and I'd lose my millions so that's a no go. Two, you have commitment written all over you. And last but not least, I don't do relationships."

Emma wasn't impressed. "You didn't have to explain any of that. I could tell the moment you opened your mouth."

Derek looked disconcerted for a moment before he recovered. "Do you have a slutty dress for tonight?"

"Excuse me?"

"There's going to be cameras, pictures in the paper and every girl that's dated Peter is gonna look at you and hate you. Don't you want that?" Derek rubbed his hands together in glee.

"Pictures in the paper?" Emma repeated.

"Didn't he tell you?"

"He said it was going to be fancy, but I didn't realize... Oh my God." She swayed.

"Hey," Derek grabbed her arm. "Don't faint on me. Peter's gonna be jealous."

Her head swam. When was the last time she ate? She stumbled and heard Derek swear. The floor disappeared beneath her feet. Lots of voices seemed to be talking at the same time. She couldn't understand any of them. Derek was snapping at everyone. What was he saying?

"Call Peter."

Derek set her on a couch and pushed her head between her knees. A chilled water bottle was pressed to her lips. She took a deep breath and took several gulps of water. Derek crouched in front of her, looking mad as hell.

"Are you sick or deathly afraid of paparazzi?" he asked.

"Neither. I only had coffee today and I guess this is all a bit... uh, overwhelming," Emma said lamely.

"Pat, a sandwich!" Derek yelled.

"I'm on it," came Pat's muffled voice.

"No, I'm fine," Emma protested and tried to stand. Her vision blurred and she sank back onto the couch.

"You do know that your boyfriend's a millionaire? If you weren't feeling well, he could have sent a limo. You didn't have to drive."

"I'm fine!"

She looked around the office. It was impressive with floor to ceiling shelves filled with books, awards and sculptures. The view behind the executive desk took her breath away. She opened her mouth to say something when she noticed a picture of herself and Peter on the desk. It was a picture that Anna forced them to take when they first began dating.

Pat handed over a ham sandwich and chips. "Is this okay?"

"This is great," Emma said and took a bite. As soon as she swallowed, the lightheaded feeling began to fade.

"You're dramatic. I'm sure there's going to be a picture of me carrying you in my arms on the Internet in the next hour," Derek said.

"You think I—" Emma began hotly when Peter rushed in.

He came straight to her. His hair was windblown as if he'd run. "Pat said you fainted. Are you sick?" He knelt in front of her and cupped her face in his hands. "Did you call a doctor?" he asked Derek.

"I'm fine," Emma interjected.

"But you fainted."

"Why the hell didn't you send her a limo?" Derek interrupted.

"Because she wouldn't have ridden in it," Peter said impatiently. "Are you sure you don't want a doctor?"

"Yes. All I had was coffee today," Emma said. "But Pat got me a sandwich and I feel better."

"Do I have to make sure you eat?" Peter demanded.

"I eat just fine. I was just a bit nervous coming here and I didn't feel like it."

"I'm going to cook this weekend and you're going to eat everything," Peter decreed.

"I carried your fair damsel through our halls like a white knight in expensive Armani," Derek added.

"He's irritating and interfering," Peter said to her, "but he kisses all the client's asses, so what can I do?"

"He's really hot," Emma said loudly.

Peter's mouth curved. "Let's make him uncomfortable."

Peter tugged her to the edge of the couch and kissed her.

He slanted his mouth over hers and his tongue entered her mouth. Her moan wasn't calculated, but it got Derek out of the office. Peter's hand brushed over her stomach and her heart jumped.

"Are you up for the party tonight?" Peter asked when they parted.

She had to take a sip of water before she could answer. "Yes."

"If you don't feel up to it, let me know. I can meet you after the party. Can you walk?"

"Yes!" she said, exasperated.

Would he be like this through her pregnancy? That actually cheered her a bit. She could bear being pampered. Even Derek reacted when she nearly fainted. Derek said he didn't do relationships, but he would probably be a great father, even though he'd gripe the whole time.

Peter put an arm around her waist and led her out of the office. Pat walked alongside them with her iPad. She ran down a list of messages, conferences and clients that needed attention. She might as well have been speaking another language. Emma's heard whirled. Peter asked Pat to reschedule some appointments and asked Pat to reply to some emails.

"I'm taking Emma home. If there's anything urgent, email me," Peter said.

Pat's mouth curved approvingly and she winked at Emma. "Yes, Mr. Logan."

"Thanks, Pat, for the sandwich," Emma said.

"No problem."

"Do you want me to carry you?" Peter asked.

"No, I felt faint for a moment. It was nothing."

Everyone was staring again. It was as if someone turned down the volume. The cacophony of the office came to an abrupt and deafening halt. She cringed when she thought of the scene she must have made when she fainted and Derek carried her through the office.

"Do you do this often or not at all?" Emma asked testily.

"Do what?" Peter asked.

"Bring your girlfriend up here."

"Never."

"Wow. I'm flattered."

"You should be. And Derek doesn't like most people, but he really likes you."

"How can you tell?"

"If any other woman fainted in front of him, he would have let them drop and called security."

"He wouldn't."

"I've seen him do it," Peter confided. "But, in his defense, some woman claimed he was the father of her baby and did a fake faint to embarrass him and cause a scene."

Emma felt her cheeks flush. "Does that happen often?"

"Every now and then. I didn't tell Derek you were coming, but he has his contacts throughout the office. He's a sneaky bastard. He didn't offend you, did he?"

She smiled. "I love him."

Peter nodded to the gaping receptionists and hustled her into the elevator. Emma felt a surge of relief when the doors closed.

"I didn't realize how big your company is. How do you handle it?" Emma asked, trying to shrug off the feeling that they were being watched.

"By coming to see you," he murmured and kissed her. "I know it's a lot, but I'm glad you came."

"I can't believe I've never seen where you work. Seeing you in a suit after being in Victoria is odd," she said, fingering the fine material.

"You don't like it?"

"It makes you look like a rich businessman."

"You say that like it's a bad thing."

The elevator doors opened and she knew it wasn't just in her mind. Everyone in the lobby was staring at them. There were several flashes from cameras. Peter kept her pressed tight against him. Six men in black suits and earpieces made a circle around them and cleared a path. They ducked into a silver car, which sped them across the street to the underground garage of his building.

"This feels so weird," Emma said.

"You'll get used to it."

Peter pulled her out of the car and led her to another elevator. He swiped a card over the keys and pressed a button.

"I don't know how I could get used to this," Emma muttered. "I didn't realize how big your company is or how well known you are. Derek said the pictures they take tonight at the party will be in the paper tomorrow."

"It's no big deal." He tried to pull her into the elevator.

"Wait, I have to get my suitcase and dress from my car."

"They've already taken it up to my floor."

"Your *floor*?" Why did she feel lightheaded again?

He typed a code into the keypad. When the doors opened Peter, looked up at a camera in the elevator and waved before stepping out. They walked down a short hall to a door with a security guard. Peter nodded to him and led Emma into his penthouse. His home was made of glass and steel. Some modern interior designer who didn't believe in comfort had decorated it. Life size glass sculptures rose out of the corners of the room and ivory and black furniture completed the remote, untouchable penthouse.

"It's different, isn't it?" Peter asked, stripping off his jacket.

"Sure is."

She stood by the door, afraid to touch anything. He strode into the stainless-steel kitchen and opened the fridge.

"Want something to drink?"

"No, I'm good," she said faintly.

It had never been more apparent how out of her league he was. He loosened his tie while taking a sip from a bottle of water and stopped when he saw her standing by the door.

"Are you going to make a run for it? What's going on?"

"I really had no idea what your life was like here in the city."

"This is the way I *have* to live in the city. It's not the way I like it, but it's necessary. Nothing's ever happened, but I have security as a precaution."

"No wonder Georgina knew who you were. I'm probably the only one that didn't know..."

"I'm the same guy whether I'm in jeans or a suit. All of this stuff just goes with living in the city."

"Mr. Logan?"

Emma jumped as a small woman came down the hallway and bobbed an old-fashioned curtsy.

"Do you need anything else?" she asked.

"No, thanks Marla. I'll see you on Monday."

Marla nodded to Emma and left the penthouse.

"My housekeeper," Peter explained.

Emma's throat felt tight as she stared at Peter and then her surroundings. He fit here. She didn't. She liked her privacy and for the first time, was grateful he never invited her to visit him in the city.

"Come," Peter said and pulled her down a long hallway.

When he pulled her into the bedroom, she was relieved to see that this room looked lived in at least. It had a gigantic connecting bathroom that was the size of the upper floor of her house. Her dress hung on a peg. Even her duffel had been unpacked. All of her clothes hung in his closet. She considered the sight and felt his hands wrap around her from behind.

"I'm glad you're here," he murmured.

She turned in his arms and looked up at him. Would her daughter have his eyes? She went on tiptoe and kissed him. This was familiar and safe. His hands tugged off her blazer and then her top.

"Are you feeling better?" he asked in a husky voice.

She nodded and he raked his teeth over her shoulder as he undressed. He pinned her beneath him on the massive bed and eyed her greedily.

"I've been thinking about this all week."

She needed reassurance that what they had was real. Peter sensed her urgency and was out of control within minutes. He plunged into her and raised her legs high so he could sink into her as deep as possible.

"Tell me you love me," he murmured.

She sank her hand into his hair, kissed him and declared, "I love you."

"God, I missed you. I'm not going to last."

"Good."

Peter laughed and then groaned. "You're going to kill me."

CHAPTER 14

While Peter cooked, he ordered Emma into a bubble bath. She soaked and stared around the grand bathroom. The look on Peter's face when he ordered her to declare her love made her heart flutter. He cared for her, but there was a world of difference between love and caring. He wanted to hear the words from her, but he never said them back.

Emma dressed in a silky robe and padded out to the kitchen. Peter talked on his cell phone as he cooked. When she heard the amount of the deal he was negotiating, her eyes bulged. Okay, yes, she was *way* out of his league. Peter made her a plate, kissed her and continued his conversation. She was halfway through her meal when he hung up.

"Sorry. Something came up," he said.

"That's fine."

He made his own plate and began to eat when the phone rang again. He grimaced, got to his feet and walked out of the kitchen. She ate in silence and heard the rumble of his voice in a distant room. She finished her meal and cleaned up the kitchen. She peeked in on Peter, but he was now tapping on his laptop while he talked and he didn't sound happy.

She wandered through the penthouse and finally walked onto the balcony that looked across the Seattle skyline. It was chilly, but she enjoyed the cold. She took a deep breath and tried to rehearse the words she would say. How do you tell a guy that you were going to have his baby? Even *normal* guys had a problem with becoming a father. What would it be like for Peter? His mom left him behind and he lived with an evil aunt who didn't care for him. No wonder he was so wary of women.

Emma walked back into the penthouse and found Peter still on the phone. She peeked into the rooms and tried to imagine dirty diapers, rattles, toys and a crib marring the high-end penthouse. She couldn't imagine a child in a setting like this. What if Peter insisted on raising the baby in Seattle? If it didn't work out and they had joint custody, would the baby have a nanny and security guards? As their child grew older, what if they chose to live in the city? She shoved away those unwelcome thoughts and began to get ready for the party.

She received a text from Anna as she did her hair and makeup.

Have you told him yet???

Her stomach lurched. *Not yet. I'll tell him tomorrow.*

Good luck! Love you!

Love you too.

Emma struck a pose when she finished. She twirled in front of the mirror. The dress fit her perfectly. She felt beautiful and not at all like a pregnant woman. When she came out into the living room, Peter was still on the phone, but he found time to get dressed in a tux that made her want to pull him back into the bedroom. When he saw her, he stopped in mid-sentence.

"I have to go," Peter said into the phone and came to her. "You look..."

"Yes?" she teased.

"Like mine," he said possessively and kissed her. His hands splayed over her bare back. "Did you bring another dress?"

Was it inappropriate? "No. Why?"

"Because Derek is going to hit on you and I'm going to have to kill him."

Emma laughed and patted his chest. "You don't have to do anything. I'm not going anywhere."

"You better not. Oh, I almost forgot."

He reached into his jacket and pulled out a long velvet box. Emma opened it and found a stunning sapphire necklace.

"I can't," she whispered.

"You can," he insisted and set it around her neck. "It matches your eyes. Now, you're ready."

"Thank you," she said and kissed him.

"If you let me, I can give you a lot more."

"I don't need anything. I just want you around more."

"I'm working on it."

Thirty minutes later, they walked into the party and Emma clutched his hand like a lifeline. How did he stand the constant scrutiny? Peter introduced her and kept her close to him at all times. She saw beyond the false smiles and sweet words to the malicious people behind the masks. It was obvious that they didn't think she was on their level and they were right. She met their stares blandly and resisted the urge to walk out. Peter was unfazed. He talked business and tried to include her in the conversation, but she was so out of her depth that there wasn't much she could contribute. The confidence she regained after they made love began to drain away. The men eyed her as if she was a brainless bimbo and her cheeks flushed. The dress she thought was so beautiful now made her feel cheap.

She excused herself to go to the bathroom and found herself cornered by a gaggle of finely dressed, catty women.

"So, you're his mistress," one said archly.

Emma raised her brows. "If you want to call it that."

"Haven't you been dating over a year? You haven't gotten him to propose?" another demanded.

"What do you care?" Emma asked with her arms crossed.

"He's going to tire of you. He always does."

"Let me worry about that. Thanks for your concern," Emma said and walked away. "Bitches."

"Do my ears deceive me or did you just cuss?" Derek appeared out of nowhere, looking handsome and sophisticated.

"Don't talk to me about cussing. I heard you swear up a storm when you carried me to Peter's office," Emma said irritably.

"What's wrong?" Derek asked, eyeing the women that filed out of the bathroom.

"Catty bitches," Emma muttered and tried to shake off her anger.

"I can—" Derek began, but she grabbed his arm.

"Don't. I can deal with it myself."

Derek cocked his head to the side as he looked her over. She grit her teeth when he circled her. When he stopped in front of her again, his eyes were alight with appreciation.

"Hot damn. No wonder they attacked you. They know there's no chance in hell Peter's giving you up."

She felt her heart lift a little. "You think so?"

"He's been warning off everyone. He might as well put a ring on you. It'll be easier," Derek said, exasperated.

Emma's heart leapt, but she reeled herself back in. Peter, married? Peter with a baby? She looked across the room at the people crowded around him, hanging onto his every word. He looked powerful, in control and gorgeous. Emma noticed a woman beside him, clutching his arm. Peter didn't seem aware of her, which meant this was a regular occurrence. The sight turned her stomach. Peter had his fair share of women, but she'd never had to face his past until now.

She couldn't imagine raising a child in the city, in this environment. There was no sign of anyone under the age of twenty-five, no sign that any of these people had children. In Bellingham, there were kids everywhere. Her little town would be a happy, safe place to raise a child. What would people say when they found out she was having a child with Peter Logan? Would they think she'd done it on purpose? Would Peter? He wanted to make their relationship work, he wanted *her*, but would he want the responsibility of being a father? It would turn his life upside down. Her stomach flipped. He barely had time for her, much less being a father.

Derek broke into her line of thought, "What did I say? Was it the ring thing?"

"Give me a moment," she said and dashed back into the bathroom.

She was grateful the stalls were empty or the women would have told Peter she was pregnant before she had a chance. She stumbled to the sink, trembling and suddenly chilled. There were handy toiletries on the counter including mouthwash. She grabbed a wad of paper towels and dabbed her sweaty face.

The strain of interacting with these people exhausted her. She suddenly wished she were at her house in Bellingham where it was quiet and she felt like herself. She looked at her reflection and though she was pale, she looked the part of a rich man's eye candy. Her hands drifted down to her stomach and she took a deep breath.

"Emma?"

She whirled as Peter walked into the lavish bathroom.

"Peter, you're in the women's bathroom."

"Derek said you were sick again."

Emma didn't want to talk to him, not now when she felt so horribly exposed and needy. "I'm fine."

He didn't look convinced. "Derek said some ladies were bothering you."

"It was nothing."

"We're leaving."

He grabbed her hand as several women walked into the bathroom and stopped, mouths agape. Peter led her back into the ballroom. She pulled him to a stop when she realized that he was making a beeline for the exit.

"I'm fine. This is just… a lot, okay?" Emma said.

"It's not okay. If you're not feeling well, we can leave."

"Do you have clients to talk to?"

He hesitated. "Yes."

"Then I'll be fine."

"Are you sure?"

"Yes." She would be damned if Derek accused her of causing Peter to mess up their business.

The night became a blur of faces, whispers and small talk. She hated it. She wished she could down the champagne circulating, but she couldn't because of the baby. People that wanted to talk business gave her pointed looks, clearly expecting her to leave, but she ignored them.

A woman named Leslie sashayed through the crowd. The slit of her dress was indecently high and her cleavage was on display for all to see. Her perfume made Emma's stomach turn. Leslie ignored Emma and pouted at Peter.

"You haven't called me," she cooed.

Peter tightened his hold when Emma tried to slide her hand from his. She wanted to punch Leslie in the face for the blatant, hungry look she shot Peter, but the potency of her perfume began to make Emma's stomach rock.

"Emma and I were on vacation," Peter said.

Leslie raised razor thin eyebrows. "Is this the girlfriend you told me about? The one that hates the spotlight?"

Leslie surveyed Emma with a sneer from her model height.

"Emma grew up in a small town," Peter said.

"That's not an excuse to be anti-social. If you want to be with Peter Logan, you need to learn how to deal with those of the same caliber."

Emma narrowed her eyes at Leslie. "And I'm sure you know everyone here."

"Of course," she said with a smile. "You know, Peter and I had a conversation about you several weeks ago. He said he'd never marry you."

Her hand in Peter's went cold and her heart sank to her toes. Peter discussed their relationship with a woman like this? All Leslie cared about was status. Emma didn't have to know about fashion to know that Leslie's outfit probably cost more than her monthly income. Emma's ears began to ring and she wanted to rip her hand away from Peter's, but she didn't want to cause a scene. Had he been seeing Leslie whenever he was in the city?

"Leslie, that's enough," Peter said coldly.

Leslie let out a tinkling laugh and gave Emma a sly wink. "If I were you, I wouldn't trust him in the city by himself. After all, the city has a lot more to offer."

The implication was obvious and Peter tightened his hold on Emma when her hand clenched into a fist.

"And when did you discuss this?" A part of her knew Leslie was trying to get a rise out of her, but she couldn't help it. She needed to know and Peter's silence was damning.

Leslie pursed perfect lips and gazed at Peter intimately.

"Two months ago? We were at a party. September four-teenth, I think."

Their anniversary, Emma thought through a haze of pain. Instead of being with her in Bellingham, he'd been at a party talking to Leslie about how he'd never marry her. The stab of pain was deep and quick. Before either of them could respond, Leslie excused herself. Peter turned towards Emma, face pained.

"You were with her on our anniversary?" Emma's voice was hoarse.

"It was a business function. She's an acquaintance."

"So, on our one-year anniversary you told an *acquaintance* you had no intention of marrying me?" Her voice was flat.

"We never discussed marriage," he said defensively.

"No, we haven't, have we? I guess that says a lot about our relationship."

"We're taking things slow. We'll see how I can move things around in my schedule and visit during the weekends. We'll see where things go from there."

Emma stared at him as if she'd never seen him before. When he reached for her, she took a step back.

"Emma," Peter began, when an older man came over and slapped him on the back.

Emma slipped away while Peter was distracted and easily lost herself in the crowd. People eyed her as if she were a leper. She didn't belong here. She hit her breaking point and made her way to the exit. A butler retrieved her coat and helped her into it.

"Is Mr. Logan leaving with you?" he inquired, concerned.

"No, he's staying."

Emma walked down the steps and hugged her coat around herself. The air was chilly and being alone made her feel marginally better. She wanted out of the city, away from Peter and his rich lifestyle. These people were so cold. How could Bellingham and Seattle be only an hour and a half away from each other, yet she couldn't relate to these people? She wanted to go home to her humble, old house and go to sleep. Maybe everything wouldn't look so bad in the morning. She thought of her car in Peter's underground garage and all the guards who would know she shouldn't be there. She could call a cab, but she had no money on her. It was late, but maybe Anna could—

"Emma?"

She whirled around. "Why do you always catch me at my worst?"

Ben held up his hands. "It's tradition, I guess. The first time we met, I pulled you out of a mud puddle."

"What are you doing here?" she demanded.

"Georgina helped me get a job. My apartment's not far from here. What are you doing?" His eyes narrowed on what he could see of her gown.

Emma fumbled. "I'm, um—"

"Going to a party?" he asked helpfully.

"Leaving one."

"Alone?"

The concern in his voice started the tear flow she didn't want or need. She held up a hand when he took a step forward.

"I'm fine. I'll see you around."

"Emma, it's almost midnight. Do you need a cab?"

"And go where?" Emma asked wildly, flinging her hands out. "I have horrible taste in men."

"What happened with Logan?" Ben's eyes fixed on the sapphire necklace.

She shot him a withering glance. "Nothing, as I expected. Why am I talking to you about this?"

"We were friends once," he said gently.

Ben was never far from her mind. He turned up in her

sketches no matter how she tried to wipe him from her memories. He'd been an integral part of her life no matter how hard she tried to deny it. He'd been her rock through school, when she started up the business and now… He was just gone from her life.

"We were friends," she whispered and couldn't stop the wistfulness in her voice. "Why did you come back to Washington?"

He shoved his hands into his pockets. "It's home."

She nodded and crossed her arms protectively around her midsection. She was in the middle of the city at midnight with several questionable looking characters leering nearby. She shifted uneasily in her heels.

"What's going on? Do you need help?" Ben asked.

Rain began to drop from the sky. Emma wrapped her coat more securely around herself. The rain came down harder, but Ben didn't walk away. He waited for an answer. She looked at him, former friend and fiancé. It couldn't be a coincidence that they ran into each other.

"You said your apartment's close?"

He nodded quickly. "Come on. This way."

Ten minutes later, she shrugged out of her jacket in Ben's apartment. It was nothing fancy and it was cluttered and comfortable. She couldn't help comparing it to Peter's home. These men had absolutely nothing in common.

"Here," Ben tossed her a towel, sweat pants and sweater. When Emma hesitated, he shrugged. "You're soaked through."

The clothes smelled of him. It was so familiar and filled her with such nostalgia, her legs buckled and she sat down hard on the couch. She buried her face in the clothes as past and present clashed together in a storm of emotion.

"Emma?" Ben sat beside her, but didn't touch.

"Why'd you walk away from me? Did you even love me?"

Emma sobbed into the clothes. "If you really loved me you wouldn't have left."

"I loved you. God, I still do but—"

"But what?" Emma shouted, raising her tear-streaked face.

Ben clenched his hands in his lap. "When I was six my grandpa and I went into the forest to cut down a Christmas tree. He lost control of the chainsaw and cut himself here." He made a slashing gesture over his belly. "I didn't know what to do. I tried to drag him back to the truck, but he was too heavy. I couldn't leave him so I stayed and watched him die."

The clothes fell from Emma's hands. She stared at him in horror. "Why didn't you tell me?"

He rose and walked to the window. "I don't talk about it."

"Six years old? I met you when we were seven," Emma said.

He leaned against the window. "You... saved me. As long as I had you with me, everything was fine. You loved me, I loved you. Everything was perfect and then the accident happened. It was deja vu. I couldn't—I'm so sorry."

Emma was stunned. Two years of hating him, of not listening and the whole time he'd been drowning in his own nightmare. When he ran a hand down his face, she saw it shake.

"That doesn't excuse me from walking away. I know that. I can never forgive myself for putting you through what I did. I should have been there. I should have fought my natural instinct to run away, but by the time I came to my senses, the ambulance had come and gone and only the police were left at the scene." Ben rubbed damp palms over his jeans. "Let me make you tea or do you want brandy?"

"Tea's good," Emma said faintly.

Ben dashed off to the kitchen and she shivered in her

thin, wet gown. She went into the bathroom and changed into his clothes. She looked into the mirror and fingered the sapphire necklace, which clashed horribly with Ben's faded sweats. She unclasped it. She would give it back to Peter. God, she looked like hell and felt like it too.

When she came out, Ben paced, kicking DVDs and books out of his way. He held out a plastic grocery bag for her wet clothes and she cringed, knowing how expensive the dress was. Anna was going to kill her. She dropped the necklace on top of the dress and saw Ben wince.

"I made peppermint tea."

Ben gestured to a steaming mug in the kitchen. Emma nodded and sat at the tiny table. He leaned against the counter as if he was afraid of crowding her. A glint of gold caught her eye and she saw her engagement ring threaded on a chain around his neck. She felt as if there was a rock in her stomach.

"Why didn't you tell me?" she whispered.

"Would it really have made a difference?"

"Yes. No. I don't know." She took a sip of tea and it warmed her insides.

"There's no excuse for what I did."

He sounded so miserable that she did something she never thought she would have the grace to do. She got up from the table and went to him. He braced himself, expecting a blow. He didn't try to defend himself. She wrapped her arms around him in a hug.

"It's okay. It's over," Emma whispered.

He was so stunned that for a full minute, he didn't return her embrace. She felt him tremble when he finally raised his arms and closed them around her. She wasn't sure how long they stood there. His breathing was ragged as he dropped his face on her shoulder. She clutched the ring on his chain.

"I don't deserve this," he murmured.

"If anyone knows how you feel, I do. You were six. I don't know how you did it. It's okay. We both survived," Emma said raggedly.

Her head pounded and she felt sick. Emotional overload. She glanced at the clock. It was past one thirty in the morning.

"Do you have something to eat?" she asked.

He laughed and pushed her into a chair. "What do you want? I have some microwaveable meals. You know I don't cook."

"Something with rice?"

He rummaged in the freezer and produced a chicken, rice and vegetable meal. He microwaved the meal, reheated her tea and made a TV dinner for himself.

"You want to tell me what's going on?" he asked.

She slumped in her chair and fiddled with a bent fork. "I don't know what you mean."

He didn't have another clean fork, so he jabbed his chopsticks at her threateningly. "Don't lie to me."

"It's... complicated."

"More complicated than the history between you and me?"

She blew out a breath. "I'm pregnant."

His chopsticks rolled across the table and he choked, "From the millionaire?"

She covered her face with her hands. "I didn't know how rich he was."

"What part of millionaire don't you understand?" he sputtered.

"Some millionaires live normal lives, right?" When he stared blankly at her, she growled, "I've never gone into *his* world. He always came to Bellingham so I wasn't prepared."

"Prepared for what?"

"Security guards, wealthy snobs, sapphire necklaces, all

his employees, his penthouse…" She massaged her forehead, which began to throb. "I'm such an idiot."

"Why?"

"We have nothing in common!" she burst out, slapping the table with her hand. "I'm pregnant and he wants to *see where things go*."

"Everyone in Bellingham expects you to announce your engagement any day now."

Emma clutched handfuls of hair. "We're nowhere near that! Tonight, at this ritzy party this woman waltzes up to us and tells me that Peter told her on the night of our one-year anniversary that he would never marry me."

"Wait a minute now, she could be lying." Ben tried to defend Peter, which made her angrier.

"He admitted it," Emma said and drank her tea. "You know, I shouldn't be angry. It's not his fault I'm pregnant and we never talked about marriage. He came after me when I tried to break up with him, but I don't think this is what he had in mind when he got me back."

"You're overreacting. Guys never voluntarily discuss kids or marriage unless the woman gives them the green light. Did you tell him about the baby?"

"I was going to tell him tomorrow." She tapped her fingers nervously on the table. "I don't want him to think I did this on purpose. That's what women do. They trap men with money!"

"So, you walked out of a party after that bitch told you this? That's why you were on the street alone at midnight in the city? Jesus, Emma. He's going to freak," Ben shook his head and finished off his meal.

"I can take care of myself."

Ben tossed their plastic plates away and pulled out a tub of ice cream, chocolate syrup and bananas.

"How can you be so blasé?" she demanded.

"You took a load off that I've been carrying around for two years. I feel great and that makes me hungry. Want some?"

"No."

She watched him make a ridiculously huge banana split. When he sat across from her and handed her a spoon, she didn't decline.

"You love him?" Ben asked without meeting her eyes.

"Yes," she said quietly.

"He loves you?"

"No."

Silence filled the small kitchen and she took a spoonful of ice cream.

"I think he'll do the right thing," Ben said finally. "He wanted to kill me at the wedding."

She rolled her eyes. "I think I stand out because I'm the only one not chasing him."

"So, what if that lady said he wouldn't marry you. He can change his mind, right?"

She looked at him. "I wish you told me about your grandpa before."

Ben paled a little. "I'm sorry. I just... I can't talk about it, even after all this time."

She nodded. She had nightmares of the bloody car accident for two years. Ben started having nightmares of blood and death right after kindergarten.

"You're going to be fine, Emma," Ben said and hesitantly placed his hand over hers. "If you and I can make it through hell, you can make it with Logan. He feels something for you."

"He feels for me, but I don't think babies ever factored in his future."

Ben shrugged. "Life throws curveballs, you can't avoid them."

"Being a grown-up sucks."

He grinned. "I know. Let's get you a cab before he calls the police."

She looked down at herself and sighed. What a bizarre day. If she could settle her differences with Ben, she could handle Peter, right? The difference was, Ben loved her and Peter didn't, so where did that leave her? Either way, she couldn't avoid this confrontation. A few hours ago, she'd been content and optimistic about their future and now... She had no idea.

Half an hour later, still dressed in Ben's clothes with her plastic grocery bag on her lap, Emma looked out of the taxi window at Peter's building. The rain came down in sheets and Ben got out of the taxi with her and unfurled an umbrella.

"It's gonna be fine. If you need me, you have my number," Ben said.

She hugged him. "Thanks."

"I love you," he said into her hair before he ducked back into the taxi.

She ran up the stairs, feeling like a homeless person as she pushed open the intimidating glass doors. What if they didn't believe she knew Peter? Maybe he wasn't home. Even as she hesitated in the lobby, Barry, the guard that escorted her across the street yesterday rushed up to her.

"Mr. Logan has been frantic, madam. He said to send you up as soon as you arrive," he said in a rush and looked her over. "What happened?"

"It's nothing. He's here?" Emma asked anxiously.

"Yes."

Thankfully, there weren't many people in the lobby. Barry led her to the elevator and pushed her inside. He typed in a code and the doors closed. She took deep breaths and clutched the plastic bag to her chest. When the elevator opened, she walked down the short hallway to Peter's front door and tried the handle. It was unlocked. She pushed the door open and saw Peter looking out the window with his back to her. It felt colder in the penthouse than it had in the rain.

"He didn't come up with you?" Peter asked in a neutral tone.

"Who?"

Peter turned slowly and she saw he held a glass with dark liquor. His movements were slow and stiff. She froze where she stood.

"Ben."

She couldn't speak. Peter was on the verge of exploding. She'd never seen him like this before. Her nerves, already stretched to the breaking point, began to fray.

"He just dropped me off."

Peter threw the glass against the wall and it shattered. Emma jumped and stared at him as muscles shifted in his face.

"I've been worried sick. I almost called the cops. I didn't know what to think when I realized you walked out of the party."

His quiet voice was threaded with such menace, her palms began to sweat.

"I've been calling your phone and watching the security cameras for hours and when I see you, you're with Ben. You don't like hearing the truth, so you leave me and sleep with him?"

"I didn't sleep with Ben!" she denied hotly.

"You come here dressed in his clothes! What else am I supposed to think? What Leslie said is true. I did say I wouldn't marry you. You and I never discussed marriage. I don't know if I'm capable of that kind of commitment. I'm trying." He turned his back on her again and looked out at Seattle. "But I don't know if this is worth it."

She swallowed the knot in her throat. "When I left the party, Ben found me walking down the street. It started to rain and since his apartment was close, I went there. He gave me his clothes so I wouldn't get sick."

"So now everything's great between you two? You forgave him for deserting you?"

"We talked. I felt it wasn't just a coincidence he found me walking down the street at midnight."

Peter turned. "So, you forgive him for all he's done, but you can't tell me where you are? Do you know how worried I was?"

"I'm sorry I walked out of the party. I just needed time." Her head began to throb and a thread of nausea made it hard for her to concentrate.

"Leslie was going for blood and you fell right into her hands. I don't pay attention to women like her. Leslie's the type that tricks you into sleeping with her just so she can claim she's pregnant."

Emma went numb. "Has that ever happened to you?"

"Yes. Since then, I've made sure it won't happen."

She couldn't tell him. Not now. These were her worst fears come true. "How can you be sure?"

"I always use protection."

But that didn't stop women from getting pregnant. They used condoms and she was on the pill and... *how?*

"I'm trying here, Emma. Are you angling for marriage? Is that why you're mad? That doesn't make sense because when I asked to move in, you panicked."

"I'm not asking for marriage. It was a slap in the face to hear you tell Leslie flat out you would never marry me on our anniversary no less!"

He let out a disgusted sound. "I can't believe we're back to this."

She blinked back angry tears. "I didn't sleep with Ben."

Peter stared at her for a long minute. "How can I believe that?"

She felt as if he plunged a dagger into her heart. "I'm not a slut."

Peter didn't say a thing. She could feel bile rising in her throat. She ran down the hallway and slammed the door to the bedroom and then the bathroom before she was sick to her stomach. A tension headache made her temples pound. She dressed in her extra clothes and repacked her duffel. She made sure she left the sapphire necklace he gave her on the bed.

When she walked back into the living room, Peter stood in the same place, watching her.

"If you walk out this time, I won't come after you," he said.

Tears slipped down her cheeks and she nodded, opened the door and closed it behind her. Her legs trembled as she walked to the elevator and pressed the button for the garage. She got into her car and despite the hour, drove out of Seattle back to Bellingham.

CHAPTER 15

*E*mma stood in front of the tombstones of her parents with her arms crossed. She shuffled her feet and murmured, "I'm pregnant."

She waited for a long minute. She wasn't sure what she was waiting for.

"The baby's father won't be involved." Almost as if she could hear her mom's screech, Emma winced. "I know, but I'm going to be fine. I know what great parents are like. I wish… I wish you guys were here. I keep thinking that one day it won't hurt as much, not having you here. I'm still waiting."

A breeze ruffled through the graveyard and her mouth curved.

"I saw Ben in Seattle. I forgave him. I don't know if we'll ever be friends again, but I'm glad we talked. I went to the cabin in Victoria. I started drawing again, Mom. I think I'll paint the walls of the nursery myself. Anna's pregnant too. We're going to deliver within a week of each other. She thinks she's going to have a boy." Emma patted her stomach. "I think I'm going to have a girl."

Tears burned in her eyes. "I love the father of my baby, but no matter what I do, it doesn't work. I haven't told him. I can't. I don't want him to think I'd do this to trap him." She brushed away the tears. "I'll tell him one day. Maybe he won't visit Bellingham for a couple of years. That will give me time. I want her to have a dad, but I don't want Peter to hurt her. I know if he's not ready, it's better for him not to be involved. I can't take it if my daughter waited up for him to come home like I have and he doesn't show. It hasn't been easy without you guys, but I'm still going. Sometimes I wonder why I'm here and you're not." She pressed her hands over her tummy. "It's because of her, isn't it? I'm excited and terrified. Sometimes I envy Anna because she has Tommy."

She hugged herself. "I stopped planning every step, Mom, and look what happened." She chuckled. "Kidding. But, I finally get it. Stop and draw the roses, yeah? I'm so tired of trying to figure everything out. I'm tired of losing people. I'm tired of being afraid to take a leap. This baby's not a mistake. She's a blessing. She's mine. One day, I'll bring her to see you. She's going to be beautiful." Tears poured down her cheeks. "I can't wait."

∼

*E*mma parked in her driveway and surveyed the trunk of her car, which contained mountains of baby stuff. She didn't want to mope about what she didn't have. In her future, there was a baby, *her* baby. She was entitled to splurge, right? She was a successful, expectant mother. She was scared and heartsick, but she was trying to change that by buying baby stuff. She didn't care that she didn't know the sex of her baby. She believed she was having a girl so everything was pink and purple.

She carried everything into the living room and was

breathing hard by the time she got everything into the house. She texted Anna who was so worried that she was driving Emma up the wall. She understood Anna's concern, but she would get through this.

To distract Anna, Emma took pictures of her baby haul. Anna sent a deluge of ecstatic texts in response. Emma began to carry the bags upstairs to the nursery. She set down her first load when she heard the front door open and close. She rolled her eyes. Anna was out of control, honestly. She attacked every baby that entered the bakery and switched between tears and screeching in a heartbeat. Emma was eternally grateful that Anna had Tommy. She wasn't sure Anna would make it as a single mother.

Emma began to make her way downstairs. "Seriously, Anna, you couldn't wait until tomorrow to see—"

She had to grab the railing so she wouldn't stumble down the last steps. Peter stood in the middle of the sea of shopping bags with a duffel in one hand. He was dressed in a suit as if he came directly from work. She couldn't read his face, but his eyes revealed he was still in a bad temper. She hadn't heard a peep from him since she left and now here he was almost two weeks later?

"What are you doing here?" she asked in a choked voice.

Peter didn't look down at the bags.

"I said I was going to clear my schedule."

For a moment, she wondered if she was hallucinating, but his eyes flicked down to the packages and she lurched into action. She made her way down the last steps to get his attention and tried to figure out what game he was playing.

"We broke up," she stated. "You told me if I walked away, you wouldn't come after me."

He shifted his shoulders irritably. "I haven't been able to concentrate."

"So, you came here for sex."

"I'm not going to say no."

She grabbed the nearest thing and came up with an umbrella. She tossed it like a spear. He sidestepped it easily. She didn't appreciate the way his lips twitched in amusement.

"Get the hell out of my house! I know you think I'm a slut, but I'm not so hit the road!" she shouted.

Peter sobered. "I was pissed that night."

Her heart pounded with longing, but she couldn't afford to do this with him. He came back to her because he couldn't concentrate on his work? "The fact that you *thought* I'd cheat on you shows how little you know me. I don't want you here."

He ran a hand through his hair. "I don't think you'd cheat on me, but I saw you with him and... I lost my mind. I mean, you said you love him!"

"I love Tommy too!"

"You weren't engaged to Tommy," he shot back.

"Peter, I'm not going to do this with you."

He took a step forward and crushed one of her bags. She let out a yelp and before he could get a glimpse of the baby items inside, tucked it under her arm. She began to gather the other bags as quickly as she could.

"Did you buy new clothes or something?" Peter asked.

"Yeah," she said in a strangled voice. She bought baby clothes.

She snatched up the last of the bags and looped the long handles over her shoulders.

"Let me help."

"No!" She held up a hand and backed towards the staircase when he came forward. "It's over, Peter."

His jaw locked. "It took me two weeks to calm down. Part of it was the fact that you left the party and let Leslie get to

161

you. The second part is I don't want Ben around you. After what he did to you—"

"He explained it to me."

"And you forgive him?"

She nodded. Peter didn't look happy about that, but he shook himself and held up his hands.

"Okay."

She took a step backwards. "Okay what?"

"I can handle that you forgive Ben. I keep trying to stay away from you, but I can't. I wish I could."

He admitted to wanting her and not being able to stay away, but he wasn't happy about it. He eyed her as if he wanted to strangle her. She narrowed her eyes at him and walked halfway up the stairs with her bags before she eyed him over the rail.

"I don't want to be around someone who doesn't want to want me."

He threw up his hands. "You think I *like* running after you like a fool?"

"You didn't run after me," she scoffed. "You took your damn sweet time. Don't let the door hit you on your way out."

She ran up the rest of the stairs because the bags were becoming heavy. She deposited them in the nursery and turned towards the door and felt her breath leave her body. Peter stood in the doorway, frowning at the freshly painted walls. He walked forward and fingered a life-sized painting she'd done of her parents on the wall.

"What's this?"

Throat constricting, she managed, "My parents."

He shot her an aggravated look. "I know that. What are you doing with this room?"

His eyes slid beyond her to the mountain of bags. She braced herself in front of them and his eyes narrowed.

"What's in the bags?"

She began to panic. "Did you know Anna's pregnant?" she blurted.

His eyes widened. "She is? No, I didn't know. I have to congratulate Tommy."

She clapped her hands together. "Yes, let's go do that downstairs."

She knew she was overdoing it, but she couldn't help it. When he started forward, she held her hands out.

"This doesn't concern you, Peter," she snapped.

"I'll determine that for myself."

He snagged one of the bags and looked inside. He frowned and pulled out tiny booties, a knitted cap and a headband. He moved Emma to the side and peeked into the other bags and looked from Emma's pale face to the baby items.

"Why are you keeping all of Anna's stuff here?"

Emma coughed. "Good question."

"She's having a girl?"

She twisted her hands. "Someone's bound to."

He reached into one of the bags and pulled out a onesie that said *Princess* across the front. Seeing the tiny outfit in Peter's huge hand stabbed her heart. Tears welled and she turned away to compose herself. She walked over to the window and saw Peter's BMW behind her car. There was an ominous silence behind her. Peter whirled her around to face him. He'd gone pale and the hand holding the onesie shook as he held it up.

"Are you pregnant?" he asked hoarsely.

His eyes dared her to lie to him. She swallowed hard and nodded. Peter staggered back as if she shot him. He looked around the nursery at the shopping bags and braced himself against the wall with his back to her. He didn't say a thing and that hurt more than she thought it would. She grit her teeth and waited. And waited. Minutes squeaked by and Peter didn't say a thing.

"I don't know if it's a girl. I have a hunch," she muttered inanely.

Still no response. She crossed her arms protectively over her stomach.

"I don't want your money. I don't need it. You don't have to be involved with the baby if you don't want to be. We never talked about kids so…"

"How far along are you?" he rasped.

"Almost three months."

"Our breakup sex?"

"Yeah."

"When did you find out?"

At least he was talking. He wasn't yelling, but his voice sounded stifled.

"The day I got back to Bellingham after Victoria. Anna came to my house. She thought she might be pregnant and she made me take a test to make sure hers was accurate. We both turned out positive."

He finally turned. "I can't believe this."

She stiffened and didn't answer. His eyes landed on her stomach and he examined her as if he'd never seen her before.

"You've seen a doctor? You're healthy?"

She blinked. "Yes."

He seemed to have trouble comprehending the latest turn in events. She couldn't decipher the look on his face, but it wasn't rage or denial so she relaxed a fraction.

"When were you going to tell me?"

She fidgeted. "I was going to tell you the day after the party."

His eyes hardened. "And after?"

"I haven't made up my mind."

He looked around the room. "You decided to go on a baby shopping spree and pick a color for the baby's room, but you didn't decide when to tell the father?"

She tilted her chin. "Do you blame me?"

He stalked forward until they were nose to nose. "Yes!"

She shoved against his chest. "How could I know you wouldn't think I did this on purpose since you think I'm a slut—"

Peter clapped a hand over her mouth and hauled her close so all she could see were his eyes.

"You don't play those types of games. I know the baby's mine."

She couldn't stop the tears that filled her eyes. His hand slid from her mouth to cup the back of her neck. He felt her tremble.

"You're not doing this alone."

The relief that shot through her system was so potent, she swayed. Peter picked her up in his arms and walked down the stairs to the living room and set her on the couch. He got a beer from the fridge and brought her a glass of water. She sipped and watched him pace in front of her.

"I'm sorry I didn't tell you," she whispered.

"Can't really blame you, can I? I accused you of sleeping around and you heard firsthand that I wouldn't marry you."

She sighed. "I don't want marriage. I never did."

"What do you want?"

She brushed away a stray tear. "I just want to be happy."

"You're excited about the baby?"

"Yes."

"Did you tell Ben?"

Surprised by the question, she frowned. "Yes."

She wasn't prepared for Peter's uproarious laughter.

"What's so funny?" she demanded.

"I tortured myself thinking of you two together when all

along, you were probably crying on his shoulder, telling him you're pregnant and that I'm a bastard."

"I don't see how that's funny."

Peter set his beer down and knelt in front of her. She wasn't prepared when he settled his hands on her tummy. She tried to move away, but there was nowhere to go.

"Are you showing?" he asked and lifted her shirt.

"Hey!"

"A little," he said thoughtfully.

Emma was transfixed at the sight of his hands splayed over her slight baby bump. Her hands shook as she tried to push him away.

"Emma, I'm going to be here every step of the way."

She met his steady gaze. "You're not angry."

"No."

"Why?"

He rubbed her baby bump. "Having a child was part of my next goal."

"What?"

"You panicked when I asked to move in with you. I was going to prove to you that I could keep my promise and be here every weekend and ease you into marrying me, maybe having a child. We're ahead of schedule."

She didn't respond.

"I know you don't believe me. That's okay. The whole Ben thing threw me off, but I can't stay away from you." He grinned at her. "Damn, I'm happy."

She never anticipated he would have this reaction. It made her throat close up and those damn hormones played havoc with her tears. While she tried to control herself, Peter framed her face with his hands and kissed her. She tried to pull away, but Peter held her still and slanted his mouth over hers. His kiss was gentle and full of comfort. He brushed kisses over her cheeks, neck and finally down to her stomach.

"I love you, Emma."

"Don't, Peter," she choked.

"Relax for me," he urged and slid his hand beneath her skirt.

She shot up from the couch and faced him, trembling. "No! You can't just come back here and say you love me because I'm pregnant. Sex won't fix what's wrong between us."

"What will fix it?"

"Time."

He groaned and dropped his head on the couch cushions. "Okay."

She crossed her arms over aching breasts. "Okay what?"

"I'll give you time."

They eyed one another hungrily. She had to look away before her self-control disappeared and she attacked him.

"I don't need to hear that you love me," she said.

"Yes, you do. I've never heard it before in my life. I need to hear it from you just as much as you need to hear it from me."

"I don't want you doing this just because I'm pregnant!" she snapped.

"You're going to be hearing me say I love you whether you want to or not. I've loved you for a while now. It took me a while to figure it out. Derek drilled it into me these past two weeks. He's gonna faint when I tell him we're expecting."

He looked so excited. Emma couldn't help the way her heart flipped.

"We'll take it one day at a time," Emma said.

Peter smiled. "You're the boss."

CHAPTER 16

*E*mma stood on the balcony of Peter's penthouse and watched Seattle get covered in snow. Her heart felt as if it was spilling over. Her coat bulged over her growing stomach and she spun in a spontaneous circle. Everything was perfect. She walked inside and couldn't stop the delighted smile that curved her mouth. The untouchable penthouse she visited months ago was gone. The modern furniture and glass sculptures were gone. In its place were comfortable couches and chairs, baby proofed outlets and drawers and roses everywhere. She walked down the hall and bounced a little as she walked into the beautiful nursery next to the master bedroom. The nursery was decorated for a princess. Peter didn't care that the sex of the baby hadn't been confirmed. He couldn't have made it clearer that he was all in.

Since he found out about the baby, Emma never spent a day off alone. Peter conferred with Anna about her work schedule and pampered her to death. Peter commuted back and forth to Seattle and though he received phone calls and sometimes had to work on his laptop, he set everything to the side when she talked. The holidays came around and Peter was with her when they went to Anna's to celebrate Thanksgiving and Christmas. Peter went to her doctor's appointments and began reading baby books. He filled her freezer with nutritious meals for her to heat up throughout the week so she didn't have to cook.

Emma tried to keep him at bay, but he wouldn't let her. He never rescheduled and when he was with her, she had his complete focus. A day never went by where he didn't say those three words. He wasn't deterred by her silence. His excitement about the baby was genuine and slowly, she began to believe in him again. He tried to convince her to visit him in the city, but she refused until now.

Emma sat on the couch to wait for him. When she heard the key in the front door, her heart skipped a beat. The door flew open and Peter stepped in. His eyes scanned the room before they fell on her. A wide smile lit his face. He came over to her, leaned down and covered her mouth with his. She clutched fistfuls of his suit and dragged him against her.

"Do you know how it makes me feel to come home and see you here?" he murmured huskily.

"No."

"I imagined coming here and seeing you like this. It feels better than I thought." He rubbed his thumb over her lip. "I love you."

She tugged and he knelt in front of her. She wasn't surprised when he spread her thighs so he pressed up against her. She cupped his face with her hands and he stilled.

"I love you," she whispered for the first time in months.

She saw the sheen of tears in his eyes before he dropped his head onto her shoulder. He wrapped his arms around her.

"Thank God. Put me out of my misery."

"What do you mean?"

169

He drew away and pulled a small box out of his pocket. He opened it up and the princess cut diamond ring dazzled her.

"I bought this after we came back from Victoria. I was going to show you I could be dependable when I moved in, but we had that fight and I went off the deep end. I don't want anyone else. You're it for me. You're having my baby."

His eyes narrowed when she didn't speak.

"You're damn well going to marry me," he growled. "You're not moving until you give me the right answer."

"I'm scared," she confessed.

"Everything will be fine once you say yes."

A gurgle of laughter burst from her. "You're relentless."

"And yours. Just so you know, I adore you." He kissed her again and it was part temper, part exasperation. "Put me out of my misery. Say yes."

"Yes."

"You won't regret it," he vowed.

His hand shook as he slid the ring onto her finger. He stared down at the ring for a few seconds before he kissed her again.

"What do you think of my new place?" he asked.

She framed his face with her hands. "It's perfect."

"Now all we need is my princess," he said, patting her stomach. "Derek insists he should be godfather. He'll teach her how to spot a prick from a mile away. I think it's a good idea."

Emma laughed. "I have something for you."

"What is it?"

When Emma just grinned at him, he scowled. "You have too much damn secrets. Give over."

She reached for the plate on the end table. He eyed the cupcake with white frosting dubiously.

"This is your surprise?"

"Eat a piece."

Slightly suspicious, he obeyed and took a bite.

"It's good." He raised the cupcake. "Why's the inside pink?"

"Because you're having a girl."

Peter choked. *"What?"*

"I had it confirmed today."

Peter leapt up and punched his air in the fist as if he won the Super bowl. Emma laughed and shrieked as he picked her up in his arms and headed to the bedroom. He set her carefully on the bed and kissed her.

"Thank you," he said reverently. "Do you have any more secrets left to tell me?"

She shook her head. "No."

"Thank God."

AUTHOR'S NOTE

Hi All,

I hope you enjoyed Emma's Secret. Please leave a review and recommend the book to a friend, it helps me out a lot!

I love romance novels. I grew up on Linda Howard, Johanna Lindsey, Julie Garwood, Jayne Ann Krentz, Nora Roberts, Harlequin novels and too many other to list here. Emma's Secret was my first attempt at a romance novel. I fell in love with the process and have been writing ever since.

I write contemporary romance, paranormal romance, and YA fantasy. I hope you'll explore my catalogue, which is full of different genres and journeys. If you're interested in signing up for my newsletter to receive news about future contemporary romances, click here.

Thank you so much for your time.

Sincerely,

AP

BOOKS BY A. P. JENSEN

Standalone:

Emma's Secret
Can't Let Go
Closure

White Mist Series:

Hell on Heels Christmas
The Songwriter
Rock Star's Ballad

Unmemorable Series:

Unmemorable
Unleashed

Cormac's Pack:

Lost in Wolf Dreams

Cursed Ancients Series:

Clutch of the Demon

Birthright Series:

Birthright
Heart of Shadows

ABOUT THE AUTHOR

A.P. loves to read, write, travel, watch movies, listen to old timer's talk about the good old days and daydream. She has two dogs who are world travelers and tolerate the long hours she spends in front of the computer.

Follow A. P. Jensen
Website
Email
Goodreads
Newsletter

 twitter.com/authorAPJensen

 instagram.com/a.p.jensen

Manufactured by Amazon.ca
Bolton, ON

29434271R00101